G R JORDAN

A Hermit's Death

Siobhan Duffy Mysteries #4

Carpetless

First edition

ISBN: 978-1-915562-84-5

This book was professionally typeset on Reedsy.
Find out more at reedsy.com

I'm a silent assassin - I can say that.

BRADLEY BEAL

Contents

Foreword

The events of this book, while based around real locations in Northern Ireland, are entirely fictional and all characters do not represent any living or deceased person. All companies are fictitious representations. Basically, it's a bit of blether!

Acknowledgement

To Ken, Jean, Colin, Evelyn, John and Rosemary for your work in bringing this novel to completion, your time and effort is deeply appreciated.

Novels by G R Jordan

Siobhan Duffy Mysteries

1. A Giant Killing
2. Death of the Witch
3. The Bloodied Hands
4. A Hermit's Death

The Highlands and Islands Detective series (Crime)

1. Water's Edge
2. The Bothy
3. The Horror Weekend
4. The Small Ferry
5. Dead at Third Man
6. The Pirate Club
7. A Personal Agenda
8. A Just Punishment
9. The Numerous Deaths of Santa Claus
10. Our Gated Community
11. The Satchel
12. Culhwch Alpha
13. Fair Market Value
14. The Coach Bomber

Kirsten Stewart Thrillers (Thriller)

Chapter 01

The weather had been atrocious. It wasn't unknown for such torrential downpours at the start of summer, but even so, no one had been out. The rain had seemed incessant, day after day, for the last four days.

Mike Doolan had been stuck in with the family. He worked from home, so on the first sunny day in almost a week, he decided he needed to get out. There were the dog, his young son, and his wife with him. In truth, Sarah had it tough, too. The young lad took entertaining. The dog hadn't gone for a walk in the rain. Therefore, the animal had tons of energy from wanting to stress out into that rain. He couldn't blame the dog; they would get soaked in an instant.

But today had started dry and as soon as Mike had seen it, he'd suggested they go to Tollymore Forest Park. Up beyond Newcastle, it was over an hour's drive away. But that didn't matter, because once there, he could take the dog out for a walk. The young lad could burn off steam. Sarah could sit down and read one of her books.

He could see her frustration, as she was snappy the night before. The weather hadn't been meant to abate until much later in the afternoon. But as forecasts usually went, it was inaccurate, and Mike made the most of it. It didn't take long to pack up the car. Sarah, of course, insisted they bring along some food as well, and they spent most of the morning in an almost empty car park.

Only a few other people had come out. Maybe that was because the clouds were still there, only breaking through to sunshine around eleven o'clock. Mike had seen a car or two roll up then, but by this point, Sarah had the cooking stove out, gas adjusted, and was ready to make the lunch.

Mike decided he'd take the young lad for a walk first. Strolling down with the boy and the dog to the river that ran through the centre of Tollymore, Mike had asked for lunch to be delayed. He told Sarah to take her book, sit and read for a bit, and he'd be back in about an hour to an hour and a half.

He walked the boy down to the Shimna River, running the feet off him, charging all the way down across the many paths that led down to the river. Once there, they were able to walk along and join the tree-lined route.

In truth, it was quite spectacular, one of Northern Ireland's best-kept secrets. You could get away from it all up here, up above Newcastle, and it was a place he remembered well.

He'd been coming here all his life, back in the days before Michael was born. Back when a proper day out was when you jumped in the car and just went, and he was delighted that today he was doing the same thing.

The dog was off the lead, walking ahead of him, and in truth, the collie was good. The boy had an outdoor passion, and they stopped a while at the stepping stones, jumping across the river, then jumping back. Mike loved the simple delight in it all, enjoying the boy dangling his feet down to the river.

Young Michael, for Sarah insisted on calling him after his

dad, was only four years old. But he was already keen to run around, a bundle of energy that had been trapped up for days. He let loose by tearing off here, there, and everywhere. Mike was having difficulty keeping up with him.

He watched as he jumped across, back and forward, from stone to stone, across a river that was still in full flow. The water was high at the stones, and Mike was careful with his son, watching closely, lest he put a foot in. But the boy was balanced, and the smile on his face made it all worthwhile.

When he'd come back to the side with his father, Mike had bent down, rustling the boy's brown hair, Michael's bright eyes looking back at him.

'Where do we go next, Dad?' he'd asked. Michael said they'd wander up, and he'd give little Michael a chance to look in a special house. The boy's eyes had widened, and he'd sent the dog on up the path. Sure, they might be a bit late coming back, but Sarah would not put the food on until she saw them. She knew him better than that.

In truth, the boy had been a surprise. Sarah and he had tried for kids for a while, and it had taken time until little Michael had arrived. It had been a tough pregnancy, and Sarah wasn't up for trying again. Mike could understand that to some degree, and he'd honoured it. But it meant that little Michael was still their only one.

Mike wandered on, looking at the trees on either side. There was a distinct wetness around and that earthy smell was everywhere. The trail had come up through both coniferous and broad-leaved woodland after they had crossed the bridge. Parnells Bridge, that was the name.

There were other paths you could break off to, but the key thing for Mike was to get up to reach the hermitage. He remembered going there as a kid. He mused on running in and imagining he was some sort of knight defending the river and all around it.

Having told little Michael he was going to approach a magical house, Mike wondered if he could let him go a little further on his own. He let the dog go with him, of course, because Tommy would stay close. *Tommy,* he thought. *Who had named the dog Tommy? Fido, Rex, something like that, surely. But Tommy?* But Tommy had been the dog's name before, and Tommy it was going to stay.

'Michael, why don't you go on up ahead with Tommy? See the house, and you can come and tell me what you found.'

It was only up and round the corner. If the child wasn't back in two minutes, Mike would go up and see what was going on. Michael took the dog's lead and Mike watched him walking round the corner, disappearing out of sight on the hard path. He could hear the boy's gurgles and laughs, the skip of his feet as he went along, and the dog's panting.

Mike turned round and looked at the river. When it was in a heavy flow, he loved it. He could hear the rush, the crash as it fell over this rock and that, and it was no different up here. He stood leaning on a piece of post, closed his eyes and let his mind drift away. The water washed over, chasing away his boss.

He had complained about him being at home. That blasted Covid, he'd said. All of you think you need to be at home now. Nobody wants to come into the office. Nobody wants . . .

Mike couldn't care what he thought. Working at home suited him, in general, unless Michael couldn't get out. Mike would take his lunch times with Michael, throwing the ball about for the dog. The three of them enjoyed themselves and gave Sarah that bit of peace. But the rain had scuppered what had gone before. Mike couldn't care less, and was only too glad to get out. He opened his eyes and looked at the river.

He's taking a while, isn't he? thought Mike. He turned and shouted after the boy.

'Michael, have you found it yet? Have you seen it?'

'I'm coming, Dad,' came a voice.

Mike turned back to look at the river. He was happy again. The boy was there. There was nothing to worry about. He looked down at the river again. He wished he could jump in, wished he could float downstream with it, just forget the day and disappear. That would not happen. Of course not. They needed to get back soon for the food.

'You find anything magical?' asked Mike, hearing the footsteps of his boy not far away. He turned and crouched down as the boy came running round the corner.

Michael had a doncher on his head, a flat cap made of cloth.

'Where did you get that?' asked Mike.

'Found it!' said Michael. 'It's cool.'

'Where did you find it?' said Mike. Not that he didn't trust Michael, but boys of that age would have stuck anything on their heads. Stick their fingers in anywhere. Heck, he might have even picked something up off the floor and eaten it.

'It's fine, Dad. There was a man wearing it.'

'A man.'

'In the magic house. Gave it to Tommy.'

'The man in the magic house gave a cap to Tommy? And what? Tommy put it on your head.'

'Oh, don't be stupid. You're stupid, Dad.'

'Why am I stupid?'

'Because Tommy can't put things up in my head. Tommy's

5

got paws. He hasn't got hands, has he? I took it out of Tommy's mouth. I put it on my head.'

'Is it dirty?' asked his father.

'Don't think so. Cool.' The child looked up at his father with a big grin on his face.

'Can I see it?' asked Mike.

'Of course. You try it on, Dad.'

Mike picked the cap off Michael's head. He pulled it up close to his nose. It was damp. Almost mildewy, like it had been out for a long time. It had been soaking wet but there was another odour from it. A foul one. One he didn't recognise.

'I think we'd better give the cap back to the man.'

'The man won't mind. The man said nothing.'

'What do you mean, "The man said nothing?"' asked Mike.

He had images of Michael, taking this cap and some poor man looking at him, too afraid to tell the child to bring it back. Maybe it was one of those people with support needs. One of those people who needed to have someone to protect them. And little Michael had run in and nicked his clothing.

'Are you sure you were given the hat?'

'I wasn't given it. I told you, Tommy had it. He gave it to Tommy.'

That was the trouble with kids. Sometimes you had to decipher what they were saying. They never put things simply.

'I think we'd better get Tommy, hadn't we?'

A barking suddenly filled the air. It sounded like Tommy. He reached down, taking Michael's hand, and asked him to lead him on round. Michael didn't seem bothered at all and led his father round the path to where they saw the hermitage. It was a stone house on the side of the river. The river flowed past it, and the rocks led down to it, but the hermitage itself, you could walk through.

An almost small cloister, the wooden walkway, allowed you to enter it in safety. Michael led Mike in towards the darkness. But from inside the hermitage, Tommy barked. Tommy wasn't a barker. He only said something if things were up, or if he was extremely agitated. Mike felt uneasy.

'Man's round the corner,' said Michael.

'Did you see him?'

'No, Dad. I told you, Tommy.'

Mike seized the lead, walking round the corner of the hermitage, through the darkness, until he could see Tommy in the corner. The dog was barking at something. The figure was hard to make out because of the lack of light, slumped away from the open windows of the hermitage, lying in the darkness. Carefully, Mike approached. Still holding Michael in his hand, as he got closer, his stomach tightened.

'Keep a few steps behind me. Okay, Michael?'

The boy nodded, doing as his father asked, and stepped back towards the entrance of the hermitage.

Mike crouched down. He came up beside the dog, who was still barking and staring at the mass in the corner. The dark mass, however, seemed to take on a more human figure. It had a coat on, but seemed to be covered up around the face, almost like the coat had been thrown round it. Mike reached forward gently and tapped what he thought was the shoulder of the figure.

'Hello?' he said. 'Hello?'

There was no response. Mike reached forward and grabbed the shoulder of the man through the coat, but there was still nothing. He reached forward, pulling the coat back and unveiled a face. It was white. Deathly white.

7

Mike stepped back for a moment, but Tommy continued to stand and bark.

'Enough, Tommy, enough!'

'Who is he?' asked Michael.

'I don't know,' said Mike, 'but can you stay there, please?'

Mike moved forward again, pulling the coat back further. The man's eyes were shut. Carefully, Mike touched his face and felt the cold skin.

'I don't think this man's very well, Michael.'

Mike thought about trying to lift the man, but when he took an arm, he found he couldn't move him such was the rigor mortis that had set in. Mike believed the man to be dead. Then the smell really hit him, because he'd realised what it was.

It had been bugging him. Mike. He hadn't worked around mortuaries or anywhere else where death happened, but he had remembered walking in on his father. His father had lain there for two days before they'd found him. It was the smell of death that was in the air.

'I'm sorry, Michael, but he's dead. We need to tell someone about this.'

'Okay,' said Michael, and he turned to walk away. Mike stood up. The man was probably a druggie. The man was probably out of his head or too drunk. He wouldn't have got caught with exposure, surely. Although if he got caught in that rain and then not got anywhere—there was no heat in the hermitage.

Mike stepped back, feeling a little queasy. Who should he ring? After all, he wasn't beside the sea, but there was a river here. Did you ring the forest ranger? Did you?

No, no, stop, Mike. Get a hold of yourself. It's time to ring the police. They'll know what to do.

8

And then he'd have to ring Sarah and tell her they were going to be delayed. Mike stepped back onto the walkway, and from there, he could barely make out the outline of the man.

'Come on then, Tommy,' he said, telling the dog to follow him. Mike took one last look, a sudden chill running down him.

Sad way to die. Ironic. A hermit dying in the hermitage. A man on his own.

He turned and followed Michael as they went back to the stones.

'Can we jump across these before we go back for lunch?'

'Oh, Michael,' said his Dad, 'we have to tell someone what's happened.'

'He's not going to go anywhere,' said Michael.

Mike shook his head. Kids were hilarious.

Chapter 02

Siobhan stood and looked out of her office window. They were finally in. The new offices in Donaghadee were established. All the painting had finally been completed.

Siobhan was firmly at home in her own office upstairs, with Julian across from her. Downstairs, Declan and Kylie had a room they could work out of, but they also managed the front desk for any walk-ins from the street. Not that there were many. Nor would the team always be in. Some days they would be shut, and people would have to call later.

But she was happy. Happy that, finally, she had a proper place for the home of her detective agency.

Siobhan stared at the name on the wall. Gold Coast Investigations. There had been some debate over the company name. Declan had preferred SD Investigations. But Siobhan didn't like that name. It gave the aura of, well, things that you picked up from being promiscuous. Yes, it purported her name. Siobhan Duffy—SD. But she thought Declan was having a dig by pushing it so much.

She wandered along her neat carpets, down the small set of stairs, and out to the modest kitchen. Behind the reception.

Declan was currently pouring himself a coffee.

'How are we going, Declan?'

'Oh, we have had nothing yet to investigate, have we?' he said. 'We had a couple of things come through that weren't really our sort of thing.'

'It takes time, Declan. At the end of the day, we can't be investigating twenty different things at once. But it'll come. Don't worry. People always have something to be looked at.'

'I thought we might get some work, Mrs D, looking into those high-profile cullings. The ones with the public officials. Seemed to me that might be something that required your skills.'

'Why would the government need me when they have a whole secret service to themselves? They also have an army. No one is going to hire me to investigate the high-profile killings of their officials. They'll do it themselves, Declan.

'We're here for private people, people who don't have all that behind them. And besides, I'm not looking to investigate killings all the time. We'll investigate robberies, break-ins, maybe even a bit of intimidation, whatever. This is a detective agency. We're not the Service. We wouldn't be advertising if we were the service, would we?'

Siobhan was thinking she might enjoy every other day—the other days when Declan went back to work in the garden. She watched him walk off, then stop and smile. Declan and Kylie were still as thick as thieves. It was nice in one way, but when you saw them every other minute of the day with his almost fawning over her—well, it was a bit much.

Julian walked in through the door, giving a broad smile to Siobhan. 'I got some donuts,' he said.

'Is that what you're reduced to?'

'Until things kick off, that's all,' said Julian.

'Declan could have got those.'

'I needed to go stretch my legs,' said Julian. 'It's fine. Until things kick off, I don't mind keeping myself busy.'

Hopefully, things would kick off soon, but you just never knew. That was the problem, thought Siobhan. And yet, she hadn't really had a moment of peace since she came back to the wee country.

As Julian walked into the kitchen to put the donuts down, the front door opened. A man dressed in jeans, a shirt, all encompassed in a rain jacket, entered quietly.

'Gold Coast Investigations,' said Kylie; 'can I help you?'

'Um, yes,' said the man. 'I need some help.'

'Well, that's why we're here,' said Kylie. 'What do you need help with?'

'Well, it's my brother. He's died.'

'I am sorry to hear that,' said Kylie. 'How can we help?'

'I'm not sure why he died,' said the man. 'The police don't seem to know as well.' The man almost turned to go away. Then he stopped again. 'I don't suppose you could help. Maybe you're not the right people.'

Before Kylie could say a word, Siobhan raced out from the kitchen.

'My name's Siobhan Duffy, and we may be able to help you. Why don't you come in and we'll discuss your issues? Can we bring you through? Get you a cup of tea, a cup of coffee.'

'Okay,' said the man. He turned and walked quietly, and Siobhan pointed him to the small office. There was a table to sit around, and the man was installed in a chair. She took his order for coffee and then passed that on to Kylie.

'Do you want me in on this, Mrs D?' asked Declan quietly in

her ear.

'Maybe; we'll wait and see what it is first,' she said. 'Don't want to spook the man with too many people in the room.'

As she said this, Julian walked past her, straight into the room, and Declan almost gave a look of, 'Well, why's he in there?' But Siobhan simply closed the door and sat down at the table beside the new arrival.

'You say your brother's dead,' said Siobhan. 'How did that happen?'

'He died up at Tollymore,' said the man. 'I don't know if you know it, the hermitage up there, by the side of the river, in Tollymore Forest Park.'

'I know it well,' said Siobhan. 'Used to go up to Tollymore as a kid. You say he died in there. How?'

'He was found dead by a walker, according to the police. They don't know why he's dead. They think he was some sort of vagrant. Possibly a drug user, but that's not right.'

'Did they say that exactly?'

'Well, they said it might have been an overdose, but Alex, my brother. He's a—well, he was quiet. A bit of a recluse, but he wasn't a druggie.'

'Can I just ask your name before we go any further?'

'Kieran Samuels. Alex Samuels was my brother. As I was saying, he had his own flat in Belfast. He was no druggie. He didn't have any particular money worries as far as I know. I don't understand it and that's what's killing me. When somebody dies and you don't know, it's hard to take. I want to know what happened to him. If it was just the cold. Why was he up there? He lived in Belfast. He wouldn't have just gone up to the Tollymore. Especially with the rain we've been having.'

'Okay,' said Siobhan. 'So, you want me to find out about your brother? And you want me to investigate? Find out how he died? We're going to need access to everything that your brother had. We can try to talk to the police, but it's not always that easy to get information out of them. You said that they suggested it might have been an overdose. Did they give you any evidence that it was?'

'Not really. "Nothing definitive," they said. I mean, I guess their people came up with the idea. CSI isn't it? That what they call them?'

'The forensic teams,' said Siobhan. 'They'll have most certainly been up there if it was suspicious. I don't know what sort of weather they were having in Tollymore. Did they say to you how long he'd been dead?'

'Several days. They said they had trouble lifting him away because everything was just so rigid. At least that's what the police told me. It's difficult getting a lot out of them. They questioned me a lot, asked me about him, but in truth, I don't know a lot about my brother. I know he lived up in Belfast, and there's something else you need to know.'

'Okay,' said Siobhan. 'Tell me.'

'According to his will, I stand to inherit half a million pounds. I don't understand where that's come from. My brother had a flat, as far as I know, although I haven't really been in it. And it's in a reasonable area, but not half a million pounds' worth. I just don't understand where he got that sort of money.'

'What did your brother do for a job?' asked Siobhan.

'Not really sure. We didn't speak that much. I didn't see him. It's all quite the mystery. I have access to his flat because I saw him occasionally and he, I think, liked the idea of me being able to go to the flat.'

'So,' said Siobhan, 'if I can clarify, your brother is found dead in Tollymore forest park. He's in the hermitage. The police are telling you he may have been a drug user, but they're giving you no evidence that was the case.'

'That's correct.'

'Well,' said Siobhan, 'we can look into it, but there are no promises. I think the first place we're going to need to start is up at his flat. If you've got access to it, that's brilliant. At least that gives us something to work from.'

'I guess most of his details will be up there. Papers, things like that.'

'Why did you choose us?' asked Siobhan.

'You're fairly local, I guess. I mean, I didn't really choose you. You see, I was walking along and I saw your signs and something clicked because you had adverts before, didn't you? I don't know why I'm in here. I just thought you could help.'

Siobhan advised the man that she most definitely could and then ran through a rough idea of the sort of charges he would be incurring.

'Well, if I'm getting half a million pounds, I should be able to cover all of that. So, I think you should look into it.'

'Gladly,' said Julian. 'We'll find out what happened to your brother.'

'Good,' said the man. He stood up, still in his raincoat, as Kylie opened the door.

'You have a cup of tea, sir,' said Kylie. She placed a couple of mugs down in front of Siobhan and Julian and the man sat back down. He took the cup of tea, his hands almost shaking, and drank down.

'What's the matter?' asked Siobhan.

'It's just all so strange. This sort of thing doesn't happen.

15

You don't end up calling people in to investigate your brother.'

'Were you close when you were younger?'

'We were, but there's only the two of us now and, well, we drifted apart a long time ago. I tried to make sure we were still talking, still had that connection. That's why I've got access to his flat, but we never really met each other. The sad thing is I'm not really sure who he was anymore, or who he became, or who did he become that he would have half a million pounds to give me. That's not all of it. There's other money going elsewhere. It's strange.'

'I'm just going to run down a few details about your brother,' said Siobhan, 'just to clarify what you've said to me.'

For the next ten minutes, Siobhan took a detailed description of the man's brother. She took dates and times of when the body had been found and of the last time that Kieran had spoken to Alex.

'I think I've got most of what I need. If our terms are okay, we'll get straight onto this,' she said.

'Just do it,' said the man. 'The money's not important. You will not bankrupt me with my inheritance coming.'

'Absolutely not,' said Siobhan. 'But we'll get started. Would you like a lift home? Julian can drive you.'

'I'll be fine,' said the man. 'I want to do a bit more walking. There's the head, you see. I don't know what to make of things at the moment. I don't know what to make of Alex. Just who was Alex? Half a million pounds? Did he win the pools or something?'

'I don't know,' said Siobhan, 'but I will find out.' The man finished his cup of tea and Siobhan walked him to the door. She caught a glimpse of Declan in the kitchen. The guy was desperately trying to listen in. As she shook the hand of Kieran,

Siobhan could tell that Declan was bursting to interrupt him, but he managed not to and Samuels went on his way.

'Right, team,' said Siobhan, 'into the conference room.'

The team gathered, Declan beaming like a Cheshire cat.

'So what we got then? Some nice juicy murder?'

'We don't know what we've got,' said Siobhan. 'The thing is that we have a man who was found dead up at the Hermitage in Tollymore. Police don't know how he truly died. We know that he's Alex Samuels, brother of Kieran Samuels, who was in with us. We also know that Kieran's about to inherit half a million pounds from him. Kieran does not know where that money came from.'

'They weren't close then,' said Declan.

'Well, obviously,' said Kylie.

'So, who do you want me to tail?' said Declan.

'You're not tailing anyone,' said Siobhan. 'First thing we're going to do is organise with Mr Samuels to get the key to his brother's flat in Belfast. We'll go there.'

'How long has he been dead?' asked Declan.

'A couple of weeks,' said Julian. 'It was just after those rainy spells that they found him. So, there'll probably be nothing much to find at the hermitage.'

'No,' said Siobhan. 'If anybody committed a killing up there, they would have cleaned anything useful away by now. We'll get a hold of Kieran and we'll get into Alex's flat. That's where we'll start. Let's try to identify who the man was because his brother doesn't seem to know at all.'

'Good,' said Julian. 'Do we all go up? Who's going?'

'I will,' said Siobhan. 'And you come too, Julian. We'll stick together until we find leads to follow. There's not much at the moment. Kylie, I want you to see if you can find anything

17

online about Kieran and his brother Alex. See what they were into.'

'What about me?' asked Declan.

'You could always go off and do the garden,' said Siobhan. She looked at Declan's face as it dropped completely.

'You're having a laugh, Mrs D, aren't you?'

'I am,' she said. 'You can join Kylie. Get us images, pictures of all of this. It makes it much easier if we have a full picture of our client.'

'Do you want me to stalk him?' said Declan.

'We don't stalk clients, Declan. They might pay us to stalk somebody else. No. We'll just go with this, okay? I'll give him a ring later on today. We'll organise a trip up to the flat. In the meantime, get on those keyboards, my warriors.'

Julian shook his head. Siobhan blushed. Her jokes weren't always the funniest, and when they didn't work, she always felt trapped by them.

'First case for Gold Coast Investigations,' said Siobhan, turning and looking at each of the others. 'Be polite. Be courteous. Find the truth. Nobody can ask for much more.'

Chapter 03

With Declan left behind in Donaghadee to mind the office, the team drove up to a swanky flat in Belfast, built within the last five years. Belfast had seen much development over the previous ten to fifteen years, and now was a city that looked very different from its past. As their car drove over the M3 overpass, routing by the home of the Belfast Giants on its right-hand side, Siobhan looked around the city. She remembered when it was very different. There were taller buildings now. Everything seemed to be on the go, a world away from when she'd grown up.

'So, how's he got this flat?' asked Julian.

'Well, Alex apparently lived here, which had surprised Kieran. Kieran had visited him in the past so he has got access. Although they talked little at all.'

'You don't find that at all strange?' asked Julian.

'I'll wait to see what I find is strange,' said Siobhan. 'At the moment, all we're going to do is check out a flat with the client.'

'You have to admit,' said Kylie, 'Kieran, he's quite good looking, isn't he? Well, in shape.'

'He's certainly well in shape,' said Julian. 'I wonder what the body they found looked like.'

'We'll see what we can get on that later. In the meantime, we follow what's in front of our nose. And that's this flat,' said Siobhan, 'so let's just get there.'

Kieran met them outside the flat, passing on the code and taking them up the many stairs, until they reached what was Alex's abode. Kieran opened the door with a key. Stepping in, Siobhan couldn't stop herself from taking a large gasp. It wasn't what she'd expected, for it was extremely elegant. If she hadn't had known better, she'd have thought it was a show flat, there to flog off the rest of the building.

'Certainly not short of money, is he?' said Julian.

He whispered this, keeping it away from Kieran, unsure whether the man would be upset by such comments. The team spread out and Siobhan got a feel for the interior. It was very well decorated, as if someone had come in and picked it all out for someone. Except there was no personalisation. There was no photograph of either Kieran or Alex.

'Kieran, you don't happen to have a photograph of your brother. Just to make it much easier.'

'I'm sorry,' he said. 'I don't. He was quite reclusive. Hard to get to know at all. Like I say, I really didn't visit him that often.'

Siobhan made her way into the bedroom, with Kieran's permission, and began looking through the wardrobe. There were suits inside, but also smart casual wear. Alex seemed like a man who would be at home out on the town. A man who could cut an image. He wouldn't be going to a Bible study or street pub. It would be in classy joints, proper restaurants, as the Belfast folk would say.

'More clothes over here,' said Julian.

Siobhan wandered over, putting her hand up on his shoulder as she gazed past him. This wardrobe was different. This was workwear, an array, different colours, from lab coats through to the rough trousers workmen would wear. Ones with padded knees. There was a myriad of boots in there, too.'

'Is that a coverall?' asked Julian. 'This isn't normal.'

'No,' said Siobhan. 'Are you thinking what I'm thinking?'

'Seen places like this before. Operator of some sort, possibly,' said Julian.

'I think we need to search this place.'

'Get Kylie to talk to Kieran,' said Julian. 'You and I can do a bit of searching then.'

Siobhan called Kylie over and then sent the girl over to Kieran. Kylie smiled broadly, looking the man up and down. He certainly looked all right.

'So you haven't been in here much,' she said.

'No, I knew little about him. I think he kept in contact because of, well, a yearning to have some sort of family about. It's all been quite a shock, what with him dying. To be honest, I don't really know who he was. I mean, look at this place—it's amazing. It's fantastic. It's no wonder he's going to give me half a million pounds, but where did he get it? Where exactly does he get all the money from? It makes little sense,'

'Were you close when you were younger?' asked Kylie,

'Not overly,' said Kieran. 'In fact, I think once we were no longer children, we didn't really speak much to each other. I was quite surprised when he came back to talk to me.'

'Well, I guess we get what we get with families, don't we?' Kylie saw Kieran looking over her shoulder.

'What are they doing?'

'Just searching. You never know what you find. Siobhan's

very good at it. So is Julian. They've been training me, but I don't have their eyes yet.'

'So what, you're like their apprentice?'

'Kind of. I say kind of. Me and Declan are maybe going to take over one day. I mean, they will not be about for more than another, what, fifteen years? Twenty, max.'

'I can hear that,' said Siobhan from the other room.

Kylie blushed slightly and gave a smile to Kieran. 'She doesn't like to be reminded of her age,' said Kylie quietly.

'And I heard that.'

'She's got some ears on her, hasn't she?' said Kieran.

'Very much so,' said Siobhan.

Kylie walked Kieran over to one of the windows and looked down on Belfast's inner city around them. It was a greyish day, which wasn't unusual, but the city was vibrant. Cars going here and there, people walking about, off to their jobs.

'Wonderful place, isn't it?' said Kieran. 'Imagine having this view every day. It would be fantastic.'

'Never mind the view,' said Kylie. 'Look at the flat. You've got all the mod cons here. Music over there. I wonder what he liked.'

Kylie pressed a button on a speaker, and classical music leapt out. It was some sort of string piece, as far as Kylie could tell. She wasn't really into classical but those must have been violins or cellos or something of that variety, surely.

'Not really my cup of tea,' said Kieran.

'Mine, neither. I wonder if he had any other stuff.'

Julian came wandering through to the room. 'What are you touching?' he asked.

'I just thought we'd put on some music while we wait.'

'Very good,' said Julian. 'Don't touch anything else.' He

22

walked past Kylie, over to the far corner of the room, and started tapping around the walls.

'What are you looking for?' asked Kieran.

'Things,' said Julian. 'Just spaces.'

It was twenty minutes later when Siobhan came back into the room and took Julian back out. Ten minutes later, she brought Kieran and Kylie through.

'We've got two hides in here,' said Siobhan. 'It's not normal as people who have hides have, well, something to hide. That's the purpose of them, but there's nothing in them.'

'Any sign they were forced into?' asked Kylie. 'Maybe somebody came in and took whatever was there.'

'No, and they were well hidden, very well hidden.'

'Maybe they were there before my brother bought the flat,' said Kieran.

'I don't think so,' said Siobhan. 'Some of it looks very new, not long installed. He's probably had this flat for a while, if you've been visiting it.'

'Well, maybe four or five years,' said Kieran.

'He's definitely had these installed. Done a great job of it, though. Peeled some of the original wallpaper back to put them in. Superb effort.'

She glanced over at Julian and gave a nod. 'I'll have another rummage around,' said Siobhan.

It was ten minutes later when Siobhan brought everyone into the front room. She sent Kylie down to get her laptop from the car, because she'd found a USB stick.

'What do you think's on there?' asked Kieran.

'Don't know. I want to make sure I can check it. Police have been here, haven't they?'

'Yeah, after he died, they came up and had a look, but they

disappeared pretty quick.'

'No wonder,' said Siobhan. 'Place looks untouched. Like he hardly lived here.'

'Do you think he did live here?' asked Kieran.

'Too many outliers. It seems to me, as with anyone like this, if he had a bit of money, he was maybe working in different places. What he was working as, well, that remains to be seen. I would have thought possibly in some sort of clandestine industry.'

'Clandestine,' said Kieran. 'I don't follow you.'

'Well, working on the quiet, trading in secret.'

'Maybe a spy,' said Kylie.

'No,' said Julian. 'I don't think he's a spy.'

'Why?' ask Kylie. 'You've got all the secret stuff, haven't you?'

'Spies don't work like this. Spies, you wouldn't know their place. They don't have anywhere that is other than normal.'

'But you two were spies, weren't you? Did you have—?'

'I had a home, but home wasn't like this. Home was very normal,' said Julian. 'Siobhan had her husband. She came back to a normal business industry. He didn't know she was a spy. My friends didn't know I was a spy. This man's advertising his wealth.'

Siobhan opened up her laptop, took the USB stick, plugged it in the side and let some software decide if she could lift off anything within it. It took a couple of minutes before she discovered there was a video file. It was large and so she double clicked it to see what was inside.

On the screen came the image of a hotel room in the middle of which was a bed. There was a man and a woman there, engaging in sex. Siobhan sat back as she watched it. 'I take it that's not your brother?'

'No,' said Kieran, 'that's not Alex. I don't know who that is. Don't know who she is either.'

'Do you know why he would have this?' asked Siobhan.

'No idea. I mean, it's . . . well . . . he's not using it recreationally, is he?'

'Most definitely not,' said Siobhan. 'If you want to do that, you can just go on the internet, can't you? Look up what you want. This looks like a blackmail tool.'

'No idea who any people are then?' said Julian. 'Don't recognise the hotel?'

'No, absolutely not. I've got no idea. I don't particularly stay in hotels.' Kieran ran his hands through his hair. He was sweating slightly.

'I think your brother is into something clandestine,' said Siobhan. 'This could very well be blackmailing. Who he's doing it for or not, I don't know. Is he a high-end operative for someone, or is he a specialist? We're going to have to look into this further. I would suggest, though, Kieran, that you don't make any noise about it, you don't ask anyone else. Can you keep yourself doing your normal things, so you don't arouse any suspicion?'

'I can, of course,' said Kieran, 'pay you for your time and just leave all this. I mean, I've got half a million coming to me. If you're telling me we could go into something dangerous—'

'That's always your option,' said Siobhan, 'and if you tell us to stop right now, we'll stop. Not a problem. We're on your pay at the end of the day so you may stop us.'

Kieran walked over and looked out the window.

'I spent my life not knowing who my brother was, seeing him occasionally, and now I find out all this stuff about him. What am I going to do with half a million, anyway?' he said.

'I'm not that sort of person. I mean, I will not buy a flat like this. Nor will I go to race off to another part of the world. If I can afford a bit to find out who he was—that's all I ever really wanted was my brother. Not everything that came with him.'

'Very well,' said Siobhan. 'We'll go now, but we will find out who he was, and who killed him.' They left Kieran to close up the flat. But as they got down to the car, Siobhan looked thoughtful.

'What's up?' asked Julian.

'It's very sloppy, isn't it?'

'Sloppy.'

'Half a million. Half a million given to your brother without telling him. No note to say I was such-and-such. A massive amount of money but puts Kieran under pressure. It invites his interest. It makes him wonder who you were, makes him want to investigate.'

'But you will not leave that note around,' said Julian. 'In case it got discovered. You can't risk that either.'

'I suppose so,' said Siobhan.

Chapter 04

'Julian,' said Siobhan, 'I want you to find out who the man and the woman in the video are.'

'Tough call,' said Julian, 'other than they're obviously enjoying the work they were doing, there are not a lot of clues in that video.'

'Indeed,' said Siobhan, 'that's why you're doing it. You can find them.'

'So, what are you going to do?' asked Julian.

'When Kieran disappears from here, Kylie and I are going to find out who rents that flat out.'

'You sure it's rented?' asked Julian.

'Oh, those are rented. You don't sell those flats. Usually, they're taken by bigwigs and companies. It's their place here if they have to visit several times a year. Firms sometimes hire them out for very special people coming over. If Alex's hiring this on his own, and if he's what I think he might be—'

'He will not have something tied to him,' said Kylie suddenly. 'He will not be wanting to sell something after he has to get out of somewhere quick.'

'Exactly,' said Siobhan. 'It also looks the part. I'm not here that often; therefore, I rent the flat. Would be strange to have bought one, unless he was some sort of megastar. He's certainly not that.'

'I'll get off then,' said Julian. He went to skip out of the car, but Siobhan grabbed him, pulled him back over. 'Take care,' she said. 'Up there's too well laid out, too neat, and too much stuff that makes me think he's in the old business.'

Julian leaned over and kissed Siobhan deeply.

'Get a room,' said Kylie from the back of the car. Julian broke off and Siobhan smiled at him. But as he got out of the car, she turned and frowned at Kylie in the back seat.

'Do you mind? He's allowed to do that.'

'Not in front of me.'

'Why not in front of you? You and Declan are out in front of us.'

'That's different,' said Kylie. 'Declan and I, well, you know, we're young.'

'Only young ones can be close like that?'

'Well,' said Kylie, 'clearly not from that video he's going to chase up.'

Siobhan turned and thought for a moment. 'Come on,' she said. 'Let's go find out more about this flat.'

Siobhan noted Kieran had disappeared, so she went to look at details about the flat. There was an inscription at the bottom saying that the entire building was owned by a management company and she quickly took down the address. Rather than drive the car into the centre of town, Siobhan realised that the office was less than a quarter of a mile away and walked with Kylie.

The management office was on the third floor of an office block building. After riding the lift, Siobhan approached the reception, asking if she could speak to someone.

'Gold Coast Investigations,' said Siobhan. 'We're looking into the death of a client's brother. The brother rented a flat from you.'

'Oh, right; that'll be Alex then. Alex Samuels.'

'That's correct,' said Siobhan. 'We've just been with his brother Kieran at the flat. He's got keys for it.'

'Oh, you've got contact details for him. That would be good. We knew that there was an extra key. We need to talk to Mr Samuels and see if he wishes to keep the flat on after his brother. It's paid up for another two months. Alex paid in advance.'

'Why?' asked Kylie.

'Because he said sometimes he was out of town.'

'Do you know what he did?'

'I best leave you to talk to Mr Bartholomew. He handles that building. He'll be here shortly.'

Siobhan and Kylie sat down on some rather comfortable chairs, waiting in the reception area until Mr Bartholomew entered. He was a squat man, not over five- feet-five, with a rotund belly and short legs. However, he had a fearsome stare over the top of some round spectacles.

'And you are?'

'Gold Coast Investigations.'

'And why should I speak to you?

'I believe you're looking to get back some keys from the flat of Alex Samuels. Kieran Samuels is our client.'

The squat man gave a nod and asked them to follow him. He led them through a busy office before stepping inside a small room with a comfortable set of table and chairs. Once Siobhan and Kylie had entered, he stuck his head out and shouted something across the office before leaning back in.

'Coffee all right for both of you?'

Siobhan nodded and watched as the little man stepped outside again. He shouted over the coffee order. He turned, came, and sat back down and waited until the coffee arrived, allowing the server to pour Siobhan's and Kylie's for them. Once that man had left, Bartholomew took a sip of his coffee and sat back in a chair that looked too big for him.

'What was he like? Alex?' posed Siobhan.

'Why do you ask?' asked Bartholomew. 'Surely, you'd know what he was like. Surely his brother—'

'His brother was not very close to him. They seemed to visit each other only occasionally. However, Alex has left a significant amount of money to his brother, which is making his brother wonder where it had come from, and he wishes to find out more about Alex.'

'There's not a lot to say about Alex,' mused Bartholomew. 'Never met the man in person. Keys were dropped off to him. Credentials were good. Paid in advance.'

'You didn't have any issues with him.'

'None. One time, there were complaints from the neighbours, but it wasn't to do with Alex, so to speak. They weren't visiting him. It's just that, a few times, some went up to his door. Alex wasn't in.'

'And these men, who are they?'

'Well, we never found out. It was disturbing for our clients, obviously. You do not buy these quality flats unless you have a significant amount of income. It's in an excellent area of Belfast. It's away from the riffraff and the last thing you need is people like that outside your door. As I say, I can't guarantee it was anything to do with Alex and when I spoke to him about it, briefly on the phone, he said he knew nothing about them.'

'Do you know what any of these people looked like?'

'We have internal footage from the building, but we don't give that out. It shows the clients' comings and goings, people visiting. We're not prepared to hand that over to someone.'

'Fair enough,' said Siobhan. 'Did the police ask for it at all?'

'The police haven't spoken to us. They spoke to the neighbours, I believe. Some of our other tenants mentioned police being round. News about Alex is slowly filtering through. Tragic accident. Don't know what he was doing all the way out there.'

'Nor do we. That's where we're keen to find out.'

'What sort of guy was he when you spoke to him?' asked Kylie.

'How do you mean?' asked Bartholomew.

'Was he eloquent? Did he speak well?'

'He spoke very well. Very polite. Assertive though. We didn't just bowl him over with terms. He indicated what he wanted and was quite happy to put up his money in order to get that.'

'What do you mean?'

'Paying up front in advance. Place was going to be unoccupied at times. He said he might be difficult to get hold of. Therefore the rent might slip.'

'Did you not just put a standing order on it or a direct debit?' asked Siobhan.

'No. Paid it off a credit card.'

'Was it the same credit card each time?'

Bartholomew looked up at her. 'I'm not prepared to give out financial details. If Kieran was here, possibly, I would talk to him about it. But I'm sorry. I'm certainly not going to pull the records.'

31

'But he didn't pay cash.'

'We wouldn't take that sort of rent in cash. Possibility of it being laundered.'

'Of course,' said Siobhan. 'However, he must have been a good client for you to allow him to pay up front and not be suspicious about why he was doing it.'

'It's his travels. Sometimes we have this with people. We don't ask too many questions about our business folk. Some of them may have—how do we put this delicately?' said Bartholomew.

'A knocking shop,' said Kylie.

Siobhan turned and looked at her and realised that Bartholomew was staring as well.

'Like a love shack,' she said. 'You know, somewhere where you take someone for sex.'

'Knocking shop?' queried Siobhan.

'Well, I thought if I'd put it in a way that maybe you older ones could understand.'

'I resent the implication that any of our flats are being used for that kind of activity,' thundered Bartholomew.

Kylie looked at him. 'Plenty of activity going on in them, isn't there?'

'He means being used for prostitutes,' said Siobhan. 'And I'll take the questions from here on in.'

Kylie's face went into a scowl.

'Sorry about that, Mr Bartholomew. Do you know anyone on your staff who met Alex?'

'When they initially started off, he was met by Crystal at the time, but Crystal's moved on. No longer in the country. Other than that, everything's been done over the phone. As we say, he's not been a problem tenant at all.'

'And you won't be releasing any of the video footage? It'd be really useful to us to know who was hanging around.'

'I appreciate it may be,' said Bartholomew, 'but I've said it before, you could see details about tenants that they don't want you to see. I'm not prepared to release that. You're not the police, after all.'

'No, we're not,' said Siobhan. 'Thank you for your time.' She drank her coffee, stood up and shook the man's hand. 'Much appreciated.'

As they left the office, Kylie tapped her on the shoulder. 'I was only saying . . . I mean, it's perfectly reasonable to think that it might . . .'

'It's perfectly reasonable, and they probably are. However, that is not what you say to the man who's running the business. That is not what you say to people. It's not what they want to hear. They're advertising luxury flats with quality people in them. Not people who have got a lot of money and use their flats for, you know, seeing somebody other than the wife or the husband.'

'But I wasn't wrong.'

'You were wrong to bring it up in that way. But no, probably fairly accurate in what you said. Anyway, it's not doing us any good. We need to find out where the video footage is.'

'Well, where would it be?'

'They must have a server,' said Siobhan. 'Central records. It will not be on physical tapes; it's going to be on a computer somewhere. We're going to have to get access to it.'

'Give me a moment,' said Kylie.

'What do you mean "give you a moment"?' said Siobhan, but Kylie was away. Siobhan watched as she stepped into what looked like a small canteen in the office. Siobhan carefully walked to a point where she could see into the canteen, wondering what Kylie was doing.

'Is your colleague all right? What's she gone in there for?' asked the receptionist.

'I think she's looking for the toilet,' said Siobhan.

'Well, the toilets are not in there. They're down that corridor.'

'I'll get her then,' said Siobhan.

She started walking towards the canteen area, but she saw Kylie emerge.

'How much is the footage worth to you?' asked Kylie.

'What?'

'How much is the footage worth to you? I can get you it.'

'From whom?'

'Young lad in there. Technical guy.'

'How do you know he's a technical guy?'

'Systems specialist. Was on his badge,' offered Kylie.

'And why is he going to help us?'

'Because he's not paid enough. He's struggling to pay his rent. And he's quite down in the dumps. Could do with a boost.'

'And you learnt this by—?'

'Using my ears. And then having a quick chat to him,' said Kylie.

Siobhan shook her head. Possibly reckless, but, at the end of the day, Kylie had found out what they needed to know.

'And where are we going to find this man?'

'Peter,' said Kylie. 'Oh, and I'm called June. You'll have to be . . . I don't know—let's say Mags.'

Siobhan raised her eyebrows, but she followed Kylie as she descended two flights of stairs to see a young man standing

34

outside a door. Kylie walked over to him.

'This is Mags,' she said. 'Mags will give you two hundred in cash.'

'Only five minutes,' said Peter. 'All of them will be on breaks. That's why they won't be here, okay? Come with me.'

He opened the door and before Siobhan stepped in, she stopped. 'Is there video recording in here? CCTV?'

'Not from this angle,' said Peter. He walked in, sat down at a laptop, and began typing in. Soon he had footage of the building.

'Is this the one you're looking for?' he said. 'It's well known because we had to look at it a lot. These are the men that were hanging around.'

Siobhan watched the footage and realised that absolutely nobody else was moving in or out of the building during the times being displayed. When Bartholomew told her he might give away secrets of his clients, he was clearly lying.

'It's quite indistinct though, isn't it?' said Siobhan. 'Is there any way to zoom in on it?'

'No, this is the footage on the files. You can blow it up, but it'll be just as grainy.' The footage ran for another couple of minutes. Then a van was seen picking up the men. Siobhan asked Peter to stop it there.

'Blow that bit up a second,' she said, pointing towards the van. The screen became fuzzier, but larger.

'What does that say?' asked Siobhan.

'Oh my, that looks like it says Markham Seafoods.'

'Yes it does. We're in business. Peter, thank you very much.' Siobhan reached into her pocket, pulled out a small wallet, and handed over two hundred pounds.

'You don't tell anyone. We don't tell anyone. Nice doing

business with you, Peter.'

The young man smiled. Siobhan saw Kylie was flashing a wide grin at him. There'd clearly been some womanly charms used in their initial conversation. To be fair, Peter looked like a man who could be taken in from a mile off.

As they left the building, Siobhan said to Kylie, 'A little heads up wouldn't go amiss next time; just tell me what you're doing.'

'It was good though, wasn't it? Got you what you needed.'

'Yes,' said Siobhan, 'and if it had of got blown up in your face and people accused you of trying to bribe someone, what would you have done?'

Kylie looked at her.

'That's why you tell me what you're doing. If it goes wrong, you've got to get back out. Well done, though,' said Siobhan, smiling. 'Well done.'

Chapter 05

U sing facial technology, Julian was able to get a rundown of who the man in the video was. His name was Randolph Fredericks. Further internet searching told Julian that the man had died of a heart attack in a London hotel. He lived in England, somewhere near Oxford, but further details were sketchy.

Julian contacted Siobhan, saying he was going to fly over to England, and suggested he take Declan with him. Siobhan agreed. Later that day, Declan and Julian caught a plane out of Belfast City Airport down to London before taking the train to Oxford.

As they sat on the train, Declan looked across at Julian. 'You can bring me up to speed, then. This guy we're going to see about.'

'Randolph Fredericks.'

'Yes,' said Declan. 'Randolph. How's he linked in with our client?'

'Our client's brother had a rather erotic video of Randolph enjoying himself in a hotel room. Later, I found out that he died of a heart attack in a London hotel. So I thought we needed to come over and find out what's been going on. He's quite a big name, Randolph, or at least was. But there's not a lot around about the hotel incident.'

'So why are we here?'

'Sometimes, Declan, if you're not being told what's what on a computer, you have to go in with your stick and you have to stir it up. I'm here to stir it up. I want to see what we can get by talking to people who are much closer to the incident.'

'Fair enough,' said Declan.

The pair hired a car once they got to Oxford and drove towards Randolph's former estate. As they pulled up beside some iron railings, Declan looked out across large lawns and a fantastic house at the far end. It was like something he would visit belonging to the National Trust.

'Flippin' heck,' said Declan. 'Look at that, I mean he wasn't short of a few bob, was he?'

'No, he wasn't,' said Julian. 'I'm wondering if we can see what they do.'

Julian pulled up by the front gate. Beyond the front gate was a small Portakabin and a man emerged from it dressed in a uniform. The gates opened slightly, and he came up to their car. Julian rolled the window down.

'Excuse me, my good man. I was wondering if I could talk with the estate management.'

'And you are?'

'My name's Julian. I'm from Gold Coast Investigations.'

'And you wish to speak to the management on what grounds?'

'I wish to talk about Randolph Fredericks. Unfortunately, I've come across something I need to talk to them about.'

'Hang on a moment,' said the man. He marched back into his Portakabin. Two minutes later, he came back towards Julian.

'I'm afraid they won't see you. You'll have to move along, sir.'

'Can I ask why?'

'I'm not privy to that sort of thing. They just said that they're not prepared to see you. Please move along, sir.'

'Go back and tell them I've discovered a video of Mr Fredericks in a hotel. A rather compromising video.'

'Have you really, sir?'

'Yes, I have,' said Julian. The man turned on his heel and walked back to the Portakabin. It was another couple of minutes before he returned.

'They're not interested. Sorry, but you'll have to move on.'

'If you could let me speak on the—'

'No, sir. I've done what you've asked. I've passed on the message. Been very polite. But at the moment, they won't speak to you. Maybe you can try contacting the office on another day. As for now, my job is to make sure these gates remain clear, and that people are either admitted or are sent on their way. I'm asking you to go on your way, sir. If you don't, I'll be forced to call the police.'

'And I might be forced to give the police this incriminating evidence,' said Julian.

'They've already answered to that. You're welcome to give it to whoever you want,' said the man. 'Sorry. The gig's up today. On your way, please.'

Julian put his hand out of the window of the car. 'Thank you for your time,' he said, shaking the guard's hand. He started the car up, reversed out, and drove round the edge of the estate.

'That wasn't very helpful, was it?' said Declan. 'What are we going to do now if they won't talk to us?'

'They're not the only ones we can talk to, Declan. Plenty of

39

other people will know what's going on.'

'Like who?'

'Like most of the people that work in there. I bet you and Kylie talk about me and Siobhan sometimes. If we've done something, gone off somewhere.'

'Of course we don't,' said Declan. 'Wouldn't dream of talking about my boss.'

'I mean to Kylie,' said Julian. 'You talk to Kylie about us. I don't mean you talk outside.'

'Oh yeah, talk to Kylie loads about you two. It's Mrs D, you see. I also wonder what Mrs D is doing sometimes. It seems to me that—'

'Well, let's just take it you do,' said Julian, cutting Declan off. 'People in here will have had their ideas and they've shared information. It's a much bigger outfit than what we're running. You'll find the people that work here permanently, they'll have an inkling.'

'Who are you going to talk to?' asked Declan. 'I mean, maybe they'll keep stum as well. That guard wasn't for talking.'

'No, he wasn't.'

Julian continued to drive, but then he saw another entrance. There were a couple of people working away on tending a small garden, moving back and forward as they worked hard.

'Useful people like me,' said Declan. But then he caught Julian's eye.

'Right, what we're going to do is you're going to go in, and you're going to ask some questions. Proper gardening questions, though, Declan. Ones that are going to need an answer. One they might have to find out. So, it's got to be to do with something you've just seen them digging. Making up a question that you're going to need advice for later.'

'OK,' said Declan. 'I think I can come up with something.'

'Good,' said Julian. 'Get him to meet us in a pub somewhere close by after he's off work. So, you can get your proper answer.'

Declan stepped out of the car once Julian had parked up and Julian watched him carefully. Declan marched up to the gate, then started shouting something through it. One gardener turned and came over. To his surprise, Julian saw Declan really engaging the farmers. There was a lot of talk. Ten minutes later, Declan came back to the car.

'Well,' asked Julian.

'Six o'clock. Dog and Duck. It's about twenty minutes from here. Didn't want to go to the closer one.'

'Is that his regular?'

'Not really.'

'And why's he going there?'

'He said he didn't want to talk about stuff from the estate.'

'What did you ask him about, then?'

'Well, I started off making a point about some of the soil and stuff he's using, where he's bought it from. But then I went into some initial ideas of disease I'd seen going around the perimeter.'

'Disease?'

'Yes,' said Declan. 'He doesn't want to talk about that in his local pub. He wants to talk about that separately. You see, the estate doesn't like people talking—really doesn't like people talking. But he's also worried that if he's got disease on it he's going to get it in the neck. So, he's talking to me in private.'

'You're a lot cleverer than you look,' said Julian.

'Is that a compliment?'

'You can take it whatever way you want,' said Julian. 'In the

41

meantime, we've got an hour or two to kill before we go to that pub. Let's go get something to eat.'

Two hours later, Julian and Declan were sitting in the pub waiting for their man to arrive. Declan sat at one table, Julian two tables further away, both quietly sipping their drinks.

Julian saw Declan stand and shake hands with the man as he came in. Declan turned, got a drink from the bar for him, and once the man was settled down and talking to Declan, Julian stood up and came over.

'Hello,' said Julian. 'I see you're speaking to my friend Declan?'

'Yeah,' said the man.

'And what's your name?'

'Andrew.'

'Okay, Andrew. Don't get up.'

Julian sat down beside Andrew. As the man went to move, Julian put a hand on his thigh. It was a pincer-like grip, holding him to the chair.

'Say nothing. We're not wanting to harm you or do anything against you. I just want to hear a rumour.'

'What do you mean?'

'We'll compensate you well,' said Julian. 'I want to know what everyone on the estate thinks happened to Randolph Fredericks.'

'He died of a heart attack in a London hotel,' said the man.

'Now, you don't believe that. I don't believe that. My friend here doesn't believe it either. So, there must have been some rumours going on about what actually happened to him. What are they?'

'I can't talk,' said Andrew. 'Got to think of my job.'

'You've just met in a clandestine place to come and talk to

us. I have no problem releasing that, telling your bosses. But, if you give me the rumours, we'll forget all about being here.'

'Well, if you put it like that, I guess a few rumours can't harm anyone. Not that I know much.'

'I just want to know what you know,' said Julian. 'Nothing more, nothing less. And just tell me if you know it or if it's a rumour. If it's a rumour, tell me how many people are spreading it.'

Andrew shook a little. He was quite a large guy, broad shoulders, maybe about six feet tall. If Julian hadn't been trained in fighting, he reckoned Andrew could take him easily. Declan, he imagined, might have been able to sort him.

'Well, it seemed strange at first, because, well, one of the ladies from the house, she said that the insurance people had been round. There was a big argument that went on.'

'Why would that be the case if he died of a heart attack.'

'His life insurance would not pay out. I think it was big. You've seen the size of the estate. They reckon he died in what they call suspicious circumstances.'

'What sort of suspicious circumstances?'

'I don't know, do I? I wasn't down in London.'

'What was the rumour then?'

'Well, they reckon he had someone in London or some women in London. He's had a clean-cut image. They try to keep a clean-cut image all about the whole estate. But there are other things that go on. Things you don't look at. But this one down in London seemed to have backfired on him. But also, he wasn't, well, I don't know,' said Andrew.

'Somebody reckoned he was, well, he was killed unnaturally in some way. A lot of rumours. The initial story was a rumour that he died. The cheerful way, someone with him, very happy.

But someone else said that wasn't true, and that's why the insurance wouldn't pay out. Somebody had ended his life.'

'Do you know that to be true?'

'That's just a wild rumour. But the thing about the insurance, that's not a rumour. We reckon that happened. That was overheard. It's second-hand,' he said, 'but it's the best I've got.'

'Good,' said Julian. 'Thank you for that. And you'll find in your lap a couple of hundred pounds. We won't be back to see you. Don't come looking for us. Just enjoy your money.'

Julian stood up, and Declan followed suit. Together, they left the pub.

'Well done, Declan. Well done. That turned out to be a bit of a win, I thought.'

Chapter 06

Siobhan drove into the small town of Ardglass, passing by Jordan's Castle. She remembered being at the rectangular tower house back in the day. Visiting the harbour town, the kids watched women shell prawns. It was picturesque and a bit of the past that always resonated with her.

Today she was looking towards Markham Seafoods. It had a small office near the harbour and from her research, she knew they sold high-end seafoods. But she wondered what on earth they were doing with their van in front of Alex's flat? Also, why were they banging on his door?

Siobhan parked up, and in a large coat and boots, marched into the front office. The man there looked her up and down, and she gave a rather terse smile towards him.

'I'm looking for the manager,' she said.

'John's out back with his staff.'

'And is John the owner?'

'No, John's the boss. He manages the day-to-day here. The man you want is Mr Markham.'

'Mr Markham would be good,' said Siobhan.

'I'd like to ask you who you are.'

'My name's Siobhan Duffy. I'm from Gold Coast Investigations. I'd like to speak to your boss about an investigation I'm running.'

'Right,' said the man, who stood up rather abruptly. 'If you sit there, I'll get Mr Markham.'

It was several minutes later when a man in a tie and jacket leaned in. 'Who are you now?' he asked.

'I told your colleague, my name's Siobhan Duffy. I'm from Gold Coast Investigations. I wish to speak to you about—'

'What do you want to be investigating us for?'

'I'm not investigating you, so to speak. I'm investigating why your van was outside one of my clients' flats.'

'You'll have to come with me,' said the man. Siobhan stood up and followed him down several corridors until a rather more swish office appeared. Inside, she was shown to a leather seat, while the man poured himself a whiskey.

'You want one?' he asked, but again rather tersely.

'I'm fine,' she said. 'One of your vans was seen outside a flat in Belfast. Several men had been out at that flat, hanging around it. They checked it out and then were taken away in your van. This is the address.' Siobhan wrote it down.

'Do you know when it was?' Siobhan wrote the date down too.

Markham buzzed an intercom, shouting at a secretary to come through. A middle-aged woman, with rather sharp-looking glasses, wandered in. He whispered in her ear; she looked over at Siobhan, almost threateningly, before disappearing back out. The man said nothing but sat there. Siobhan could hear a clock in the background ticking away, making the silence even longer.

The door opened. The secretary marched back in, and

placed a sheet of paper in front of Mr Markham.

'Had no vans out at that time. Don't know what that's about,' he said.

'Really? So, people are able just to take your vans?'

'Vans are locked up at night. Locked away. He must be mistaken. Must have been a different van. Markham. Larkham. I don't know. Something like that. Certainly wasn't us.'

'I'm not looking to implicate you in something. I'm just trying to find out who these men were,' said Siobhan.

'Well I wish you good luck because we don't know them at all. As far as we know, our vans were in. We can tell as well because we note the speedometer count. If we note what is down there, nothing's out of order. Must have been somebody painted our name on it. If you find them, send them my way, because I'm not happy about that.'

'What is it you do here exactly? Seafood?'

'What's that meant to mean?' asked Markham.

'They were outside the front of my client's brother's house. Watching his flat. Men jumping out, running around.'

'Told you it's got nothing to do with this.'

Unbeknownst to Markham, Siobhan was reaching into her coat pocket. A hand inside her pocket, she pulled out the smallest of devices. She stuck it underneath her chair extremely casually, waiting until Markham was at his angriest before doing it.

'Well, it seems suspicious to me. I think I'll be back,' she said. 'Thank you for your time.'

'No point coming back, as we don't know anything,' he said.

Siobhan left, made her way home, and joined Kylie. That night, the two of them watched a film and after taking a call from Julian relaying the information he'd picked up, Siobhan went to bed a happy girl.

The next day Siobhan travelled to Ardglass again. Markham entered the small office she was now in, but instead of inviting her to his own, he stood there, hands on hips.

'I've told you; we don't know a darn thing about that van or where it's come from. Just clear off, okay? Not interested. Not interested in you coming back. Not interested in you giving us grief about something we've nothing to do with. So just clear off, okay?'

'But you haven't answered my question. You haven't told me why your van was there.'

'Piss off, okay? Just piss off, woman. Don't come back in here. Next time, we'll have to throw you out. Well, I can't say it'll be me. It might be somebody a lot more aggressive than me. If you catch my drift.'

'Catch your drift perfectly,' said Siobhan. 'See you around.'

She made sure that her boots clipped across the hard floor as she left. He'd be in a pickle now. A panic, wondering when she'd come back. She walked out to her car, parked a short distance away and then switched on the other end of the small device that she'd put on the chair the previous day. This was a receiver, and she sat with a pad of paper ready to make notes. It would record it all, of course, but Siobhan liked to make notes. It made you think about something as it was happening.

It was about half an hour before the office of Markham became an interesting place. She'd heard the door open and close several times. Footsteps come into the office. And then she heard him make a phone call, buttons being pressed as he dialled out.

'Manfred. Got a few of us here. We got a problem.'

'What sort of problem?' said the voice from the other end of the line.

He said, 'Well, some woman goes by the name of Siobhan Duffy and describes herself as being from Gold Coast Investigations. Seems to me she's digging around. She saw the van that time it was outside the flat.'

'The one in Belfast with Manfred. The one that—'

'Yeah, that one, the one where the guy died up in Tollymore. Yeah.'

Siobhan was amazed, they were talking on the phone, but they were sharing things that most everybody knew. Clever, not letting anything out that shouldn't be.

'Did she say anything?' asked Manfred.

'Said she'd be back. She said she'd be interested in us. Should I get some of the boys to go round? Teach her not to poke her nose in.'

'No. The boys will come back with a bloody nose. You need to leave her to me,' said Manfred. 'She knows how to handle herself. But so do I. Sit tight, do nothing. I'll be in touch.'

'What do I do if she comes back here?'

'Wait it out. Say nothing. Sit tight. Okay?'

The conversation ended, and Siobhan smiled to herself. She had them where she wanted them. She just needed to keep stringing them along.

Chapter 07

J ulian was not someone who particularly liked London. It was the claustrophobic-ness of it all. Everyone on top of you. He may have been from England, but he certainly wasn't from its capital. He found it to be in squalor often, and he struggled with those sleeping on the streets.

These days, of course, many of the big cities had a similar issue. Even Belfast wasn't immune to it. But London was just somewhere he struggled with. There was such money being spent all around him. And yet here, there were also people without. No doubt there were people trying their best to change that, or to help with it as well as they could. As he strode along the street, heading for one of the major insurance firms in town, he was having trouble reconciling the world around him.

But as much as Julian felt everything, he displayed nothing on his face. He had to fight to stop himself from saying a hello or good morning to everyone as he passed by. It was a habit he'd picked up in Northern Ireland, where everyone seemed to say something to someone else, even if it was only just about the weather. He thought it was not a bad habit. At least it kept people feeling like they were part of something, connected in some way.

He left Declan back at a hotel. The people he was going to see, he would have to be specific and quiet with, not so enthused as Declan became. Julian wanted to give the image he was still working for the service, not that he was part of an independent investigation. The people he would speak to would talk to people in the service at least, giving up a little information for the country. At least that's the way he used to play it.

He was dressed in a smart suit. It was dark, but there was a blue tie running down over a crisp white shirt. It was over formal, worn not out of choice, but because of the occasion. Something Julian resented. He liked Siobhan's style, dressed fairly casual, often in her jeans and her jumper, no happier than just wrapped up in a blanket.

Julian thought of her as he walked along the street. He hadn't imagined that when he retired from the service, he'd end up in so much trouble. He'd rather have settled down more with her. But the nature of the woman was that she needed something to do. She needed something to investigate. She needed to be in the middle of some sort of action. And if she found a cause, she wouldn't back down. He wouldn't be finding her on a golf course, playing away the rest of her days. It wouldn't entertain Siobhan.

He went through the revolving door of the tower of offices and made his way across the lobby over to the lift. Stepping inside, he pressed the button for his intended floor, and saw another group of hands come and press theirs, before everyone stood perfectly still.

There was one conversation going on at the back, but it was distinctly private. The mirrored interior of the lift made it look larger than it actually was, but Julian felt everyone around him. He was good with his sense of smell and being this close with people who had just walked far through the city wasn't a great place to be.

When the doors opened and he could step out onto a fresh landing, he took in a deep breath and still found the air somewhat stale. Regardless, he marched on and soon came to the offices of McClintock and Sons.

'Hello, my name is Julian and I'm an old pal of Howard's. If you could just let him know Julian's here.'

'Julian who?'

'That's correct, Julian.'

Julian turned away from the receptionist and sat down, picking up a magazine, opening it, but sat without looking at it. He stared across at the office suite, hoping that the receptionist wouldn't ask any more questions, but simply get hold of Howard.

She stood up, and disappeared for a moment. Then she came back to say that Mr McClintock would be with Julian presently. Julian sat, flipping the pages of the magazine as if he was reading it, but watching all those around him. It was a force of habit, something he developed in the Service, where you never knew when you were being watched.

Would he be watched now? He doubted it. He didn't feel as if he'd had people tailing him since he'd been on the mainland. But you didn't develop automatic practices because of what you knew; it was because of what you didn't know and what would catch you out.

No one came to mind as Howard McClintock strode through a pair of double doors with his large hand outstretched.

'Julian, old boy, what about you?'

It was a phrase that Howard McClintock had picked up when he'd done some work in Northern Ireland with Julian. Of course, he said it wrong. He formalised it. The phrase was "'bout ye!"

'No bad at all,' said Julian. 'Thank you for seeing me.'

'One of our finest. Of course I'll see you. Not a problem. Come in. Come with me. You go through to my office.'

Julian was led by Howard into a rather sumptuous office at the far end of the floor suite. As he stepped inside, Howard closed the blinds to the office and then pointed to a large drinks' cabinet on the far side.

'Too early in the day for you?' he said. 'Would you rather have coffee?'

'Coffee would be better,' said Julian. 'I don't drink as much as I used to.'

'Due to time, or because of your own decision?'

'Own decision,' said Julian.

'Ah, you've got a woman then.'

Julian laughed. 'Is it that obvious?'

Julian would never have refused a drink in case he would have offended, even at this time of the morning. He was getting out of the habit.

'Are you still working for them?'

Julian looked over at Howard and shook his head. 'No,' he said, 'I'm not. I'm still working, just not for them. Started up my own.'

'Good,' said Howard. 'Make a bit of money, eh? Government pays you nothing. Remember that from my days of being tied to them. Still, it was a secure job back then, though yours wasn't that secure, was it?'

Julian laughed. 'Can I ask you—'

Howard put his hand up. 'No, not yet. I'll get the coffee through first.'

Julian looked a little surprised until Howard said that, given the questions Julian had asked him in the past, he'd rather they got asked to just him and not before somebody passing through. Julian found this funny, as if Julian would ask a question that couldn't be heard by someone in the room without any wrong actions being taken. A couple of minutes later, Julian had a cup of coffee in his hand, which tasted rather fine. Clearly, Howard didn't skimp on what he got.

'So then,' said Howard, leaning forward at his desk, 'what can I help you with?'

'Does the name Randolph Fredericks mean anything to you?'

'I thought you'd come with a more difficult one than that. Randolph Fredericks means a lot to anyone in the insurance game.'

'Why's that?'

'Well, it was the big story. The man who died of a heart attack in a hotel. A hotel where he was without his wife, and without most of his entourage.'

'Something funny going on with it?' asked Julian.

'Something not funny went on with it,' said Howard. 'Let me elaborate. Randolph Fredericks. Owner of a small fortune. Has a habit of annoying people though with his acquisitions and takeovers. Although he tries to present a very family-friendly image, at least the estate did, he was also a man who took what he wanted. And the rumour was that he took too much down in that hotel and had a heart attack.

'So why all the speculation? Why all the shouting and getting on? Well, the trouble is,' said Howard, 'we weren't convinced, or at least the industry wasn't convinced. It passed through several people. When it started, because of who he was, they obviously wanted it to be well looked at. But the doctor who certified it was very suspect. One of Randolph's own, so they decided instead to bring in an independent one. But there were a lot of rumours about how independent he was, and if he'd been got at. I mean, this is more your stuff,' said Howard. 'Back in the day, you'd have loved all of this.'

'Back in the day was a while ago,' said Julian. 'Why did you suspect something else, though? That sounds a bit more than just a family messing about.'

'Well, the family may mess about anyway, but Randolph was also an assassination threat. The insurance company, well, they wanted to make sure it wasn't an unlawful killing. A killing of any sort.'

'And there was suspicion?' asked Julian.

'There was great suspicion. He was away without his protection. One bodyguard around him. A bodyguard that strangely got fired not long after that. Or rather, we think he got paid off, told to shut up, and not come back.'

'Well, that's certainly strange,' said Julian. 'Were you able to prove anything?'

'They fought hard. Really hard. Took a long time for the payout. But the police report said it was a heart attack. The coroner looked into it. Came back with a heart attack.'

'What was your take on it?'

'If I had to put my money on it,' said Howard. 'I'd have said he was taken out. Everything said coverup. The way the family went about it. A lot of money to be lost. Awful lot of money to be lost. That's part of the problem. But they couldn't prove anything. I mean, Frederick's estate get their hands in everything. It's why if somebody wanted to do something to them, it would be a top hitman, hitwoman, whatever. Somebody who would understand it all, be able to close in quickly.'

'And he was definitely away doing what he shouldn't have been doing?'

'Almost definitely, but the heart attack bit, I didn't buy it. He lived life to the full, but he wasn't unhealthy. Fredericks was in a good place in that sense. He wasn't that old; it just doesn't work for me, I'm afraid.'

'The hotel where he died?' said Julian.

'Relatively new one,' said Howard; 'the Starling. It's pretty good actually—stayed in it myself. Although obviously not using it for the same recreational reasons that he was. But it's classy, upmarket, and that's why he went there. They wouldn't say anything. You know what it's like in this field; you've got to have people you can trust, especially guys like that, if they want to play around.'

Julian knew it all right. He'd tailed plenty of these people before; some with strange habits, some who just were getting away from it all.

'If I show you a bit of film, can you tell me if it's the hotel room?'

'I only saw a couple of pictures of it when I was asked to consult,' said Howard. 'So I'll try, but no guarantees,'

'What you're going to see may be a little . . . how shall I put it?'

'Fun?' said Howard,

'Well, yes.'

Julian took out his phone, played the video that had been found inside Kieran's flat.

Howard sat back. 'Well, that's him. I don't know who she is,' said Howard; 'never been with her.' He gave a grin. 'I'm actually a much more settled man these days. I'd be a bit like yourself.'

Julian smiled back, but all he wanted to know was about the hotel room. 'What about the room?'

'Yes. That's the Starling,' said Howard.

'Well, thank you,' said Julian. 'You've been immensely helpful.'

Howard stood up, came round behind his desk, and put his hand out to Julian. 'Any time, but as usual, nothing came from me.'

'Of course,' said Julian. 'You know that.'

'Since I've told you something I shouldn't, you can tell me something you shouldn't.'

'What's that?'

'Who's got you into a state of not drinking? Who's got you? Thinking about what you do instead of just doing it for what the job requires?' asked Howard.

Julian took out his phone again and clicked through until he got a picture of Siobhan. He showed it to Howard.

'Seen her before,' he said.

'With me once. Embassy do, I think it was,' said Julian. 'She was with my group; she wasn't with me.'

'Well, looks good for you,' said Howard, smiling. 'Anything else you need, anytime. Good to catch up with an old friend, though. You take care of yourself.'

'And you,' said Julian.

As he walked out of the building, he checked to make sure no one was watching. He made sure that nobody would come for his friend Howard. That was the trouble, Julian thought, with this business. Everywhere you go, everyone you talk to, all that ever runs through your head, is trying to make sure that nobody harms them afterwards.

Chapter 08

Siobhan Duffy sat in her car, listening to the conversations between Manfred and Markham Seafoods. He mentioned her several times, saying he was looking into her and she was getting slightly worried.

Siobhan had left Kylie back to mind the office, and she had a few different people come in. Most of whom she couldn't put down as being from the Seafoods but there were certainly some questions being asked. She'd been able to help none of them in terms of taking on a case, but from Siobhan asking her questions, it seemed that they were certainly being watched.

However, it seemed to Siobhan that Manfred was finding out nothing about her, and he talked about other operations that were going on. Meanwhile, Siobhan had been into the company several times. Each time, she did the same thing, getting told to piss off in no uncertain terms. Although once it had graduated to the F-word.

Siobhan was delighted, for they seemed to take great offence at what she was doing. She was under their skin, and when you get under people's skin, they get rattled and they make mistakes. She just had to wait for it.

It was late in the afternoon when Siobhan heard the call

from Manfred. 'Need to see you,' said Manfred.

'About what?'

'That woman. We need to talk about her. Talk about what she's after. She knows too much. I think she must know about our friend.'

Siobhan did not know who 'our friend' was, but she was definitely interested.

'Where do we meet, Manfred?'

'Usual place. Tonight. Midnight.'

'Okay.'

'And don't be late. If you're late, it might be your last meeting.'

'Hey, I won't be late. You know I won't. She's the one causing the problem, not me.'

'You got spotted. Your crew got spotted. You're causing me a problem. Be there.'

Siobhan placed a call to Kylie, advising her she'd be working that night and to go straight home, and then to get herself out to Ardglass. She didn't want to lose sight of the man from Markham Foods. She was watching until the business closed.

Siobhan tailed him back to his house when he left and sat a little way off, waiting for him to come out that night. Kylie joined up with her and they sat in the car, pondering what was going on.

'Julian phoned,' said Siobhan. 'He's done well. Looks like Fredericks was involved in an insurance case after he died. Seems like he may have been killed unlawfully.'

'So where does that get us?'

'Not too far at the moment,' says Siobhan. 'Julian's going to chase it down further though.'

'Julian and Declan, you mean.'

'Julian. Declan's there to assist. You two still need to get into your heads that you're not equals in this business. You don't have the skills; you don't have the experience.'

'And yet I am here in your car helping you.'

'Yes, at the moment. Make sure you listen. Make sure you do as you're told. These guys we're messing with here, I'm not sure that we should be messing with them.'

Siobhan thought Kylie had seen enough so far to know not to get out of hand. But she got very enthusiastic and sometimes thought she was better than she was. A true spy, a real operative, knew what they were, knew what they were like. And while they may have had confidence, they made sure they stayed well clear of their limits.

'There he is,' said Siobhan as the man from the Markham Seafoods left his house and got into his car. Siobhan tailed him from a distance until she saw him disappear out to a house in the country. He drove down the driveway, parked up, and from the road a distance off, Siobhan saw him step inside the dark house. She parked her car further up.

'Right, we're on foot,' said Siobhan. 'We'll have to get up close and then I'll try to get in.'

'Do we need anything with us?'

'Like what?' said Siobhan.

'Well, like, maybe a gun?'

'Guns are bad news,' said Siobhan. 'I only carry guns when I truly need them.'

'Well, what if you don't know you need them?'

'Then you have to think of something else,' said Siobhan. 'I won't carry a gun, just for the sake of it.'

'Can I carry it?' asked Kylie.

'You don't shoot well enough. You're liable to kill somebody innocent.' Kylie looked round, almost laughing, but saw that Siobhan was deadly serious.

'Put your head together,' said Siobhan. 'This isn't a joke, this one. You've got to be careful.'

Siobhan got out of the car and jumped over a fence into a field, approaching the house away from the road. As they got closer, Siobhan had them both lie down in the grass, binoculars focused on the house. 'There's no light,' said Siobhan, 'but there definitely are people moving about.'

'How do we get in?' asked Kylie.

'We?' said Siobhan. 'We don't get in. I get in.'

'And what, you leave me out here on my own? That doesn't sound good,' said Kylie. 'How do I know if you're all right? How do I know if you need help? How do I—'

'If I need help, you won't be worth anything. Because the help I need will be serious help.'

'What, you're going to leave me out here? Too easy to get spotted and caught, surely. Especially with my untrained abilities.'

Siobhan weighed this up. There was something to keeping Kylie close, yet she wondered why she'd brought her at all. But the woman needed to learn, needed to get close to such danger, needed to understand her limits. And then one day, when she was good enough, she may take this all on herself. Besides, Siobhan sometimes needed backup, wherever it came from.

Siobhan approached the building down low, Kylie beside her. It was now into the darkness of the night, which was short-lived because of the summer, but Siobhan knew how to use the darkness.

Creeping up close, she stopped at the rear door of the house, listening intently. Siobhan turned it once and found it open. She stepped inside into a kitchen. It was old style, with pots hanging from the ceiling, what looked like an aga on the far side. But she wasn't stopping to admire the kitchen. Instead, she crept silently across the room, listening in at the far door, where she could see a light filtering out underneath it. She held her finger up to her mouth, showing that Kylie needed to be quiet.

'You need to take care of it,' said a voice. She recognised it as Manfred. Carefully, Siobhan cracked open the door slightly. She peered in and could see someone standing there. She wasn't sure it was Manfred or not, but there was money in his hand.

'If we finish her, there'll be a bonus in it. We need to keep her away, okay? We need to make sure she doesn't come round again.'

Siobhan could see money changing hands, but she wasn't sure quite what was being said. She turned back to look at Kylie. As she did so, she was aware that the rear door was just slightly open. She hadn't left it that way. Kylie had closed the door behind after her. Kylie wouldn't leave it that way, thought Siobhan. She'd be too careful. She'd be too afraid of what Siobhan would say. Carefully, Siobhan turned and grabbed Kylie by the collar, pulling her down and out of the way.

'What's up?' whispered Kylie.

'Did you shut the door? Properly.'

Kylie nodded. Siobhan pointed to it. Somebody was about. Somebody was close.

'How do we catch them?' asked Kylie.

'We don't,' said Siobhan. 'We get the hell out of here. Now.'

63

She grabbed Kylie as she went to run. 'But slowly and quietly,' she whispered. Siobhan crept across the kitchen and then raced back as the rear door opened. As she made her way across the kitchen, she reached up, pulling a knife out of a wooden rack sitting on the side. And then in the darkness of the dining room, just beyond the living room door, she stared at the man who had walked in.

He was large, robust, and certainly didn't look like he would be up for any sort of negotiation. He looked left and right, and then he marched on towards the dining room. Clearly, he must have known whereabouts they were. He just had to find their exact location.

Siobhan didn't give him the chance. She leapt out, plunging a knife into his shoulder. He cried out, and she was already grabbing Kylie, throwing her towards the door. Suddenly, there was a cacophony of noise inside the meeting next door, as Siobhan turned and ran, desperate to get away.

Kylie was at the door, urging her forward, but Siobhan saw a hand slip around Kylie's mouth. She turned, and as the door into the living room, where she'd seen the money being exchanged, was opened, she threw a knife at it. It slammed into the wood in front of the face of a rather disturbed individual.

Siobhan legged it through the door, looking for Kylie, slamming the door behind her. A man was dragging Kylie at this time, but he was slow because of it, and Siobhan ran to catch up with him. He tossed Kylie to the ground with one simple flick of his wrist. Siobhan couldn't take long, and yet the man was a brute.

She lunged forward and feigned that she was going to kick him down towards the knees. He bent down, and she put her hands together, swinging as hard as she could, both fists intertwined, catching him across the jaw. He stumbled backwards but would not go down. As he did so, Siobhan grabbed a pot with a plant in it and flung it towards him. The man didn't see it coming as he raised himself back up, and out of the darkness, a large pot cracked onto his head. He lay there, shaking.

Siobhan turned to Kylie and grabbed her hand, pulling her up to her feet. 'Go,' she said, and together they ran for the fence that cut off the grounds of the house. Siobhan threw herself over it, but Kylie caught her foot in it, tripping her up and making her tumble to the ground. Luckily she was clear, and Siobhan saw figures exiting the house at pace.

'Go,' she said to Kylie, 'go!'

Together, the two of them raced hard through the fields and out towards Siobhan's car. As she got there, Siobhan could see another car pull up behind it.

'Stay here,' said Siobhan to Kylie.

'What are you going to do?'

'I'm going to have them run after me. As soon as I do, you get in our car, and you leg it too.'

Kylie looked questioningly at Siobhan, but the woman was already away, creeping up quickly and quietly behind the other car. Two men had come out of the car and gone to investigate Siobhan's.

Siobhan crept carefully, slowly opening the door and then jumping into the driver's seat. As the car started, the men suddenly looked back, and Siobhan was already reversing. They ran towards her, and she drove straight at one, clipping him on the side as he dived out of the way.

He lay on the ground, wincing as Siobhan drove off, but the other man took off after her. Siobhan let him stay close, as if

65

he was liable to catch. She began to step on and off the throttle, slamming the brakes occasionally, as if she was a woman that couldn't drive. She kept up this fiasco until she was sure that Kylie was in her car.

The man tailing Siobhan turned round to see Siobhan's car racing towards him. Kylie never swerved, and the man ended up diving out of the way. Siobhan raced off in the man's car, quickly followed by Kylie.

Siobhan looked for a decent bend in the road and when she got to one, she drove the car up towards the edge. Looking at where it would tumble down, she opened the car door at a low speed, before jumping out. She was sure the car had enough momentum so that it would roll off the edge of the road and drop down the small cliff.

As Kylie pulled up, Siobhan jumped into the car beside her. 'Where to?'

'Let's not go home,' said Siobhan. 'Hotel. Tomorrow, I think we're going to meet the boys.'

'Why? What's up?'

'I need to talk to Julian. I'm not sure how deep we're getting in here, or what we're getting ourselves into. He'll know. He'll have a good idea.'

'And I'll rack up the air miles,' said Kylie. Siobhan looked across at her, her head shaking. 'What? I've got to get my flights away somehow.'

Chapter 09

Julian got Declan to wait in the car while he went to approach the hotel. He told Declan to be lookout for anyone suspicious following him. He had seen no one, and he didn't really count Declan as being able to spot anyone either. However, it meant he had somebody in a car waiting to go if he needed to get out of there. The Starling was indeed impressive, modern in style, and as Julian entered the lobby, he saw a bustling hotel. He sat in the corner watching the comings and goings before making his way over to the reception desk, speaking to the attendant there.

'I'm here from Parsons Insurance. We're re-looking into the death of Mr Randolph Fredericks. I'd like to talk to your management if they have a moment.'

The man behind the desk looked truly impressed and disappeared, before bringing to the desk a much older man. He stared with eyes of disgust at Julian.

'It's all been settled and done,' he said. 'That was the whole point when we got everybody together. You don't get any insurance out of this anymore. Nothing there to be claimed for. Randolph Fredericks would have had it all sorted, anyway. It's the type of guy he was.'

'Well,' said Julian, 'I'd like to ask some questions. To the management.'

Unfortunately, they didn't seem to want to answer them. It was a quick wave of the hand and Julian saw he was being approached by two rather large gentlemen.

'This insurance man is about to leave. The business is done and dusted. It's more likely you're a hack.'

A large man stepped forward to grab Julian by the arm, but Julian hurried it out of the way, moving in behind the large man and pressing into his neck. 'That's enough,' he said. 'I don't need to do a lot, but I have you at my mercy. I'll be going.'

The man flinched, and Julian turned to walk away. He heard footsteps after him, but he put a hand up, and whoever was coming towards him was told to back off. As he stood outside on the street, he glanced over at Declan. The young man was still there, watching intently behind his newspaper.

Julian thought about getting Declan made up in a proper outfit. Some sort of driver's uniform. Julian could be the lord behind him. Except it didn't work with a lot of the places they went to. Why would people like that even be looking at the Starling, except to stay there? They certainly wouldn't be asking questions.

Julian decided he needed a different approach, so he disappeared around the rear of the hotel, watching the staff. As in any hotel, there were those that seemed to be on next to nothing. Most of them seemed to be foreign people, new to the land, and any of the English he heard being spoken was not clear. They couldn't be second generation or third generation in the country. He saddled up beside one who seemed to be particularly forlorn and fed up.

'I'd like to have a chat for money,' he said.

'Chat for money,' said the man. 'I don't understand.'

'I chat. You tell me what I want to know. I pay you money.'

The man looked around him quickly. 'You need the money?' asked Julian. The man nodded and pulled Julian round the corner.

'What is it you want?'

'I want to know what happened, all about Mr Fredericks.'

'Everything happened,' said the man.

'Everything?' Julian pulled some money out of his wallet and handed it to the man. 'Maybe your memory comes back in a more detailed fashion,' he said.

'I'm just a cleaner. I take the sheets and boil them, yes? But what I heard, you want to know.'

'Tell me,' said Julian.

'You pay me first.' Julian handed him a fifty-pound note. The man shook his head. 'What I've got is worth a lot more than that.'

'Well, I won't know until you tell me,' said Julian. 'I won't have a clue what it's worth.'

'Fredericks didn't die the way he was meant to.'

'All right. Is this a vengeful thing, or was someone just working their way up?'

'Randolph, the important man, Frederick's, he would come and there was a special woman. They would go in there and they would, you know, get it on. Well, this time he doesn't come back out. And when he didn't come back out, I never saw the body, but I was asked to go in and clear out the mattress.'

'What was special about the mattress?'

'Two bullet holes. The holes were side-by-side. I don't know if there was much else in the mattress. Our mattresses have coveralls. We have sheets that protect the mattress. So, maybe,

69

when he was shot, that's where the blood went. I didn't do the sheets. I was asked to move the bed.'

'And you say the holes were side-by-side,' said Julian.

'Totally. Right side-by-side.'

'How far apart?' asked Julian. The man indicated with his two fingers.

That's a double tap, thought Julian. *That's somebody making sure he's dead.*

'When they told you to move the bed, what happened to it?'

'Was taken away. Destroyed. Burnt, I think.'

'Were you here when it happened? When they found him?'

'Yes,' said the man. 'But they didn't ask me to do the bed right away. There was a lot of panic. A lot of rich people were telephoned. People were spoken to. The body—they didn't move it for a while.'

'That's interesting,' said Julian.

'And since then, I don't know. Has anyone said anything?'

'We don't talk to anyone. But they don't pay me well either,' said the man. 'If they paid me more, maybe I'd have stayed quiet. But they paid me nothing. Just told me I could lose my job.'

Julian reached into his pocket, took out a couple of hundred pounds, and handed it to the man. 'Thank you,' he said. The man turned and walked away. Julian was going to walk back out towards the car, but as the man stepped inside the hotel again, Julian thought he saw somebody watching him.

Quickly, Julian tore to the door that the man had entered by, opening it. He looked down the corridor, saw the man, but someone was also behind him. The man was moving in the quick, easy style that an operative would, hunting prey, ready to take it out.

70

Julian effortlessly moved down the corridor behind him, then slipping into an alcove before watching the pursuer disappear round the corner. He was about to follow him when he saw a second man. He wouldn't have given him much of a thought, except he signalled the first one, and made off down a different corridor.

Pincer, thought Julian, *they're going to bring them in together.*

He headed down after the second man, pursuing him in what turned out to be a maze of corridors on the ground floor of the Starling.

Julian could hear words from the man up ahead. 'What do you want?'

There was silence in reply, and then there was a shriek from the man. He had turned, as far as Julian could tell from his footsteps, and was now running towards him. Of course he'd get caught up by the other man, and Julian saw the second man pulling a knife out, stop at a corner, ready to deal a blow.

Julian stepped forward quickly, kicking into the back of the man's leg, forcing him down to the ground. As his informant ran past, the man looked at Julian in terror.

'Get out! Don't come back to the hotel. Just keep going. Get lost,' said Julian.

The man had been knocked to the floor, and was now turning round to slash with his knife. Julian stepped back once and then launched a kick towards the hand, which was awfully close to the wall. He connected, the hand cracked into the wall and the knife dropped.

Julian casually gave him another kick to the chin, and the man fell backward just as his friend arrived. This time, there was a gun out in front of him. But Julian was quick, slapping it to one side and driving two fingers into the man's throat.

71

He gurgled, stepping back, and Julian grabbed his arm, smacking it off the wall. He followed this up by twisting and then driving an elbow into the man's stomach. The man doubled up and Julian elbowed him in the back of the head before driving his head into the wall. Stunned, the man rolled about, collapsing as Julian turned away, walking quietly and efficiently out towards the exit.

It was as he was going he heard the voice of his informant again. He was almost screaming, and Julian ran hard. As he turned round a corner, he saw three men now holding the man. One had him tight, another was up in his face, trying to extort information from him, while a third was standing there watching him, with a gun pointed towards him. Julian swept round the corner, and before anyone could react, he went straight for the gun. He grabbed the hand that was holding it, turned and pointed it at the other man in front of his informant.

'Stand down. Sit on your hands. Hurry up,' he called.

He then swung the gun in the hand between the two men interrogating his informant and then told his informant to get out of there. The man turned with no hesitation and ran for his life. Julian watched closely, careful to try to keep everyone at bay by using his gun.

The man whose hand it was in was woozy, and Julian drove another elbow into his stomach. He reached over, took the gun from the man's hand, and pointed it at everyone.

'I'm going to go,' he said. 'Don't follow me. Not a single one of you. You'll be all right.'

He walked along the corridor, pointing the gun at them. They all stood there, arms wide, as if he was holding the most powerful weapon the world had ever seen. As he got to the double doors behind him, he figured he had another corner or two, and then he was out to the street.

He held the gun through the double doors, waiting until they were almost closed before slipping in behind them. He then turned, took a handkerchief from his pocket, and as he walked along, wiped the gun, replacing his handkerchief.

Julian saw the bottom of a laundry chute and flung the gun in there. Stepping as quickly as anyone, he walked clean out of the building, towards the car that was waiting. He stepped inside and told Declan to put his foot down.

'Trouble there?' asked Declan.

'Something went on, Declan, I'm convinced of that now. All we've got to do is work out what and who.'

Declan nodded. He drove as quickly out of London as he could.

Chapter 10

Siobhan stepped inside the small country hotel and saw a familiar face at the bar. She wanted to run over, throw her arms around him, hug him tightly, but something said that she needed to play it carefully. So she walked up with Kylie and checked into their rooms. She took a key and when they got there, she dumped her bags on the bed, telling Kylie to throw hers on the twin bed beside.

'Let's go see them,' she said. Kylie followed her back through the hotel to the bar. Together, Kylie and Siobhan sat at one end of the bar, while Julian and Declan were at the other. Slowly, Julian made his way down and turned to the barkeeper.

'Can we get a couple of drinks for these ladies?'

'Maybe I'm not that type of girl,' said Siobhan.

'Sure, you'll take a drink from a decent man like myself?'

Siobhan laughed and gave a nod. A few minutes later, they'd taken up a seat in the hotel lounge's corner. It was quiet, very few other people were about. She went and clocked the place first to see if there were any familiar or lurking faces and there were none. She gave a nod to Julian.

'Where are we at?'

'Well, from the sounds of it, you've been chased off, just like us. I'm worried,' Julian said. 'Could be disturbing some big fish with this one.'

'Indeed,' said Siobhan. 'But I don't understand it. We go to investigate someone who's died. They've left half a million to their brother. They don't see their brother very often. Where's this half million come from? It's like he's turning into being some sort of hitman.'

'That's what it's looking like,' says Julian. 'Randolph Frederick's estate seemed to do a cover-up about how he died. But clearly there was some sort of hit involved. Somebody got to him. I don't know how or in what way. But he never left that hotel alive. And the heart attack story's made up. It was confirmed by a guy at the hotel. It's also confirmed by Howard, my friend, in the insurance industry. They just couldn't prove it.

'But he's dealing with somebody big enough that they are able to get the police on side. The reports came through that he died from a heart attack. Yet there's two bullet holes in the bed. For real? Forensics don't miss that.'

'Did forensics get the right bed?' asked Siobhan.

'I think we've been observed though,' said Kylie. 'Trying to see who we were. I had some people come by the office, checking us out.'

Julian looked worried. 'Anything more than that?'

'They were wise enough to check if we were listening. I walked into it. Yes, I got us out, but I think we're dealing with people who are better than they should be. This isn't some amateur firm running out through the fish exporters. Markham's is just a small part. Manfred, the guy behind it, the guy who seems to be organising them, I don't know who he is, but he knows how to operate. Much smarter.'

Julian looked away for a moment and Siobhan felt she needed to continue with her thoughts.

'Well, is Alex more than he seems then? This Alex who doesn't seem to be anything or was possibly a businessman when we saw his suits. Is he actually some sort of hitman? Or is he a fixer? Maybe that's it, except—'

'The outfits in his apartment make little sense,' said Julian, 'if he's a fixer. They don't get all the gear. The smart stuff, yes. But they don't get their hands dirty.'

'So where are we at?' asked Siobhan. 'How do we take this on?'

'Should we take it on?' said Julian.

Siobhan stopped for a moment, looking over at him. 'What do you mean, should we take it on?'

'What I mean is, should we be taking this on? We're a detective agency. This is treading into territory that is well beyond that.'

'Can I speak to Julian alone?' asked Siobhan quickly.

'No, you don't,' said Julian. 'Declan and Kylie have a say in this.'

'That's right, Mrs D. Julian's talking about why we should be involved in this. We have a right to that conversation.'

'Or we can just have the conversation. Keep them out of it,' said Siobhan.

'Them is here in the room,' said Kylie. 'And them would like a say.'

'Shush,' said Siobhan.

'She's correct,' said Julian. 'And you're trying to shush her because you want the decision between you and me. You need to put it to the four of us.'

'Put it to the four of us? I'm the boss here,' said Siobhan. 'I can keep them out of it.'

'No,' said Julian. 'They're already hanging around the office. Whatever we do, they will be at risk, too. This has to be a decision by all of us to go further on this.'

Siobhan flexed her fists. She'd been chased off and had to get out quickly. She'd arrived desperate to see Julian. Desperate to have an intimate chat with him. To be held by him. To be reassured again. And straight away, he's talking about throwing the case.

'I know it's not in your make-up,' he said to Siobhan. 'It's not. But that's why you need me here. You need the voice of reason. You need someone who's going to tell you when you're being ridiculous.'

'I'm not being ridiculous. We're following up a case.'

'That we are at the moment.'

'I'm the one who nearly got Julian killed,' said Declan. 'Who got you and Kylie into trouble? You!'

'We're a detective agency and we're going to get into trouble. We're not just sitting here seeing whose husband's running off with who.'

'Are you bottling it?' said Siobhan.

She looked over at Kylie, who looked down, and at Declan, who looked down. But when she looked at Julian, he was staring straight back.

'No,' he said, 'you're not doing that. This is not about pride. This is about a sensible decision. We're not the service. There is not a problem, an issue that we must sort out. This is not for the good of the country, not for the good of someone else. This is someone who has come along, paid us, and said get involved in this and tell me what's going on. At the end of it, the win is we get some money. Not, the country is once again safe.'

Siobhan's lip went up on one side. 'The trouble is,' said Siobhan, 'is that something is going on.'

'And we don't know why we're involved in it. We don't know where it's come from. We don't know if Kieran knows more than what he says. So, we need to tread carefully,' said Julian. 'In fact, if we tread at all.'

'It's nothing too bad that we can't handle.'

'Excuse me,' said Julian.

'If I could just point out, Mrs D,' said Declan, 'that while I'm happy to work for you, we're actually holding this meeting in England. We work out of Northern Ireland. We're not meeting there because we're not safe. Things happened before where we weren't safe, but we at least knew what was going on and some of them we couldn't do anything about. We've taken this one by choice and without really knowing anything that's going on, and we seem to be getting a lot of attention.

'If you don't mind me saying you've had fifty years; I still have a good time to go. Maybe living off a pension won't be good for you, but I'd like to get there. I'd like to share that pension with Kylie.'

'What?' said Siobhan. 'Why are you talking about pensions? We've got a case; it's in hand here at the moment. We have a—'

'Stop,' said Julian. 'Stop. Vote if we go on.'

'What?' said Siobhan. 'It's not a vote. It's a—'

'Vote if we go on. You've pulled those two into it. They're at risk now. We need to assess the risks. They didn't volunteer to be in the Service. They volunteered to be in a detective agency. In fact, they didn't volunteer. You're paying them to be. You have a duty of care to them. It's far beyond what the Service does. Or did.'

'Right, then,' said Siobhan. 'Who wants to continue with the case?'

Siobhan raised her hand slightly. So did Kylie and Declan, surprising Siobhan. Julian had his hand firmly down.

'Why are you saying no?'

'It doesn't feel right,' said Julian. 'This does not feel right at all. Something is up with this case. Something smells. And we're getting a lot of heat from people who haven't got a lot to be worried about.'

'Well, we're still in it. So let's kill this idea of whether or not we're going on and decide what we're going to do,' said Siobhan.

'The way I see it,' said Kylie, 'is that we don't know enough. And we haven't got enough. You haven't got very many places to go to find anything else out. I mean, you've gone down your line, Julian, and it's ended up saying that something's not right. But it hasn't given you a lot of leads though, has it?'

'That's correct,' said Julian, 'if not so eloquently put.'

'And you, Mrs D, what have you come up with? You've got chased because some guy called Manfred basically has nicked somebody's van.'

'Thanks, Declan,' said Siobhan.

'There's nothing else, is there?' said Julian. 'We haven't come up with other ideas to run down.

'We could investigate our client,' said Siobhan.

'We could, but, well, we did our best,' said Declan, ' and that's what we've been trying to do.'

'I'm not getting anywhere,' said Julian. 'The trouble is also, we're now clocked. They know you; they know me.'

'Not quite,' said Declan. 'There's a group back in Northern Ireland. They know Siobhan; they know Kylie. They don't know me, and they don't know you. And the group here, in England, well, they kind of know you, Julian. They might have seen me in the car. So they possibly know me too. So I think there's an obvious solution.'

'Really, Declan?' said Siobhan.

'He's right,' said Kylie. 'We just swap targets.'

'Swap targets?' blurted Siobhan.

'And we close the office,' said Julian.

'We cannot close the office,' said Siobhan. 'We're not that long open. Everybody's going to look and think Gold Coast investigations—they don't open at all. That's why I've had Kylie staying.'

'If any of these people want to send a message, and trust me, when I was in the hotel, somebody was trying to send me a message. They weren't too shabby about pulling a gun, but if they want to send a message to us, whoever's in that office could get on the wrong end of it. You and I might see it coming. These kids won't,' said Julian.

'Who you calling a kid?' said Declan.

'You. And Kylie,' said Julian. 'And she knows it.'

'Who's she, the cat's mother?' said Siobhan.

'Don't start that,' said Julian. 'Stuff the language. You know what I'm saying's right. You cannot put these two at risk. And you cannot afford to have you and me,' said Julian, 'in that office.'

Siobhan looked over at Declan and then at Kylie. They were good kids. They worked hard. It would come as a crushing blow to them to be told that they couldn't do something on their own. But Julian was right. If somebody wanted to make a point against them, they were the two that the point was going to be made against. One of them would suffer. Maybe even lose their life. Siobhan wasn't happy that she understood her foe well enough at the moment.

'We close it for the minute,' she said, 'until we understand who we're up against and why we're up against them. When we do, we'll open again. Julian, Declan, head back to Northern Ireland. Declan, you pick up investigating Manfred. I stay here with Kylie and look at Randolph.'

'Good idea!' said Julian.

'That's the way we work it. Good, let's move on. That's sorted.' Siobhan stood up and walked off towards her room. Kylie went to get up, but Julian stopped her.

'I will go,' he said. 'Declan and I are on the way tomorrow. You two have an evening together. Get yourself some dinner here. Don't go out. Do whatever you kids do in your room. Use Declan's and mine. I'll stay in with Siobhan.'

'Is she going to be all right? Is Mrs D going to be okay?' asked Declan.

'Unfortunately, sometimes in a relationship,' Julian said to Declan, 'you have to actually talk sense and not just pander to what the other person wants so you can make them feel good. Siobhan is a wonderful person, but she's a stubborn one. And she gets the bit between her teeth for a case, and that's it. Too often so far, that's nearly ended up costing us. This isn't the Service. She needs to learn that. Unfortunately, I'm the only one that's going to tell her.'

He turned and walked off, leaving the two younger people behind.

'What do you want for dinner?' said Declan.

'Room service,' said Kylie'

'You don't want to eat down here?'

'You daft idiot. I want room service . . . and served by you!'

Chapter 11

Siobhan smiled at Kylie. 'Looks like today is going to be an internet search and library day. That's what you're good at.'

Kylie didn't look back, but had a rather sombre look on her face. Siobhan knew what the problem was. They'd just taken Declan and Julian to the airport. They were returning to Northern Ireland to follow up the Markham Seafoods lead.

'It's all right, they'll be there when we get back,' said Siobhan.

Kylie looked distant though. Siobhan wondered how last night had been. Last night with her and Julian had been interesting, to say the least. She always thought Julian would back her up in what she wanted to do. But that wasn't the case. It was probably a good thing.

They always said that in the Service, you needed someone who would turn around and tell you when they thought you were wrong. Then did it when you made your decision. That's what Julian was doing. But she could tell he was worried. They'd got into big stuff before.

And Kylie and Declan were getting better. They weren't as green as when they first started out. But then again, at that point, she hadn't brought them in. They were just there, tagging along. And that wasn't a case. That wasn't a proper organisation. She was just trying to look out for an old friend.

'Better get to it,' said Kylie. She sat down in front of her laptop and Siobhan stepped away to sit on the bed with her own.

Randolph Fredericks was an interesting bloke, thought Siobhan. His estate, much more interesting again. He seemed to have fingers in so many pies. But what interested her was he had a foundation that helped unfortunate kids from an estate in Londonderry. The city with two names depending on which side of the fence she sat on. At least, that's how it had been.

Siobhan read the article in front of her, paying close attention to exactly what the foundation was doing. The brochure, lifted by PDF onto the laptop, explained how certain kids were being chosen to blossom their acting and dancing talent. It seemed to be a good thing, endorsed by several celebrities. Siobhan couldn't find anything that looked wrong in it. Not until she clocked that several kids went away to one of Randolph's estates for personal tuition by the best dance teachers.

Of course, there was nothing wrong with that, but that wasn't what you did these days. You had a much more hands-off approach. That being said, to go away to the estate that the Fredericks owned would be quite something. But Siobhan was wary. Extremely wary of anything that might give an opportunity to carry out actions that would not be seen in broad daylight.

'You finding anything on these charitable works?' she asked Kylie.

'Got several things.'

'Anything in Northern Ireland?'

'Something about an estate up in Derry?' said Kylie.

'That's what I got as well. How do you think it looks?'

'It all looks fine and legitimate.'

'That's the only link to Northern Ireland. Let's have a look there. Let's investigate this charity.'

'Why?' asked Kylie.

'Because all the action apart from Randolph's killing has taken place back home. I know we're over here, but any action over here apart from the killing has been instigated by ourselves. It's just a hunch,'

'Do you want me to keep going on other things as well?'

'One thing at a time,' said Siobhan. 'Besides, it'll get you back over the water to see Declan again. That's why your face looks like a smacked arse, isn't it?'

Kylie stuck her tongue out at Siobhan and went back to her laptop for a moment, before she turned and looked. 'What Julian was saying—he doesn't seem keen to go on with this.'

'He's doing his job, decision's made, and he's doing his job,' said Siobhan. 'It's what we all do now, do our job,'

Kylie turned back to her laptop, began tapping in on the keyboard again, before she turned back. 'He's quite an excellent judge, though, isn't he?'

'Julian's a brilliant judge. That's why he's on the team, not simply because he's my partner.'

'So why do you disagree with him?' asked Kylie.

'We have a job to do. I don't think this is as dangerous as he thinks.'

'But why? Is it because you're letting your feelings get in the way? Because you want to get after this person. To find him. To—'

'Kylie, how many bosses have you had before?' asked

Siobhan. 'You don't judge the boss. You don't turn round and actually ask them questions like that. I've had years of experience. I value Julian's opinion more than you'll ever know. But I don't agree with him on this one. As I'm the boss, that's what we're doing. Find me some details about this charity of the Fredericks.'

Kylie turned back, her face looking sore again. Siobhan put down her laptop.

'I'm going out for a moment. I won't be long.'

Siobhan stepped out of the room and went down to the bar area. It was early in the morning, still only about nine o'clock, and the bar wasn't open. But she got a coffee and sat by one of the windows of the hotel. There was a pond outside with some ducks in it. The hotel was nothing particularly swish, and that was the whole point. They were getting away, making sure they were well out of the danger zone.

Was she playing this too close to the bone? The trouble Siobhan knew about herself was she was used to the danger. She'd spent her entire life running around people with guns. People who might kill you. Professional people. And she'd even seen hitmen in her time. She'd not been on the end of one, though.

Siobhan was never that important. Not really. She was a cog in the wheel. Now, however, she was the boss. That changed things. If they came, was Julian right? They wouldn't come for her or for Julian. They'd make a statement. Take out the secretary in the office—whoever was there minding the desk.

She sighed. It wasn't an itch, Siobhan knew it. There was something in her that was desperately keen to take on the big stuff. To be relevant, needed.

She sat back in the chair. She had what she wanted now, didn't she? Her place by the sea. She had her house looking out into the waters. Out where the ferries would first come round to meet the loch.

Siobhan had her paradise. She wanted everything. Julian. After all these years of not really loving a husband, of not being with Eamon, she had a man she truly wanted. And yet here she was, running off, looking for more action and adventure. Was he not adventure enough? She never settled down, did she? Instead, she started her own agency. And she dragged two novices into it. If Julian hadn't been there, would she have continued? He had got her out of a few scrapes, after all.

Siobhan looked across at a man sitting at a table, enjoying some scrambled eggs and bacon. He kept glancing over at her. Was he some sort of spy for the people they were investigating? Was he monitoring her? Had they been discovered even here?

No, she thought. He's got that look. He's interested in me. Oh well, she thought. Better than being from them. Better than a tail.

She finished her coffee and went to walk away, but had to go past the man on the way to the door. As she did so, he suddenly stood up. She felt her hands tense.

'Excuse me,' he said. 'I know this is terribly forward and you're about to—I'd probably disappear off out of the hotel, but I couldn't help but notice you. Quite frankly, you've taken my breath away. I was wondering, would you want to stay for a coffee? Can we have a talk? I'm not a weirdo, I'm just, my name's Alan, and the—'

'Let me stop you there, Alan,' said Siobhan. 'I'm attached. I've got a partner, but that's very sweet of you. Now I need to go.'

The man looked embarrassed, and Siobhan felt for him. She walked beyond him, and wondered to herself, was that an act?

Was that someone trying to get under her skin. Trying to see what she was actually doing regarding the investigation. Or was he genuine? Was he just wanting to say hello? Did he really find himself besotted with her?

She wanted to believe the latter, but the former might have been more likely. Siobhan didn't return to her room and instead watched him. The man seemed lonely, somewhat sad.

He went back to his room and came out later with a packed suitcase. He drove off in his car. And Siobhan stood at the window of the hotel watching him go. It then hit her.

A moment like that, quite exhilarating. When somebody suddenly thinks you're wonderful enough to stop you on first sight, to want to get to know you more, and then all she thought about was who they were and why there's somebody coming to either watch her, or even kill her.

The Service did that to you. The Service she'd worked in for years. But so did this. So did running her own business in this line of work. She was about to go back up to Kylie, but she ordered another coffee and sat down again.

Should she be in this line of work? she thought. *Was it good for her soul, for her mental health, for her physical health?*

She was going into her fifties now and, after all, she didn't feel quite the same as she did when she was younger. Yes, she was no relic, but she wasn't as sprightly as before. When things got hurt, they remained hurt for a lot longer.

Was Julian right? Was it this doggedness, this bloody mindedness, that was making her charge in? Was it the thrill of it all? And where did the thrill not become a thrill at all?

It was an hour later when she walked back up to the room. She opened the door and looked over at the seat where Kylie would have been, but there was no one there. She looked around quickly. There were no signs of distress. Everything looked normal.

Siobhan heard the bathroom door open to the side of her and she caught something out of the corner of her eye coming down towards her. She reached up with her hand, grabbing the nightstick as it descended. She twisted the assailant's arms, throwing them onto the bed. And then she stopped and stood, watching Kylie complain about her wrist.

'What are you doing?' asked Siobhan.

'You were gone for a couple of hours,' said Kylie. 'I thought they'd got you.'

Of course, thought Siobhan. *You did, didn't you? Why wouldn't you?*

'Sorry,' she said. 'I was distracted. I was just having coffee downstairs. In fact, I was not quite propositioned, but well, a man asked me if I wanted to sit with him and talk.'

'One of the people from the case.'

'No. Totally random person. I have to say, it was different.'

'Did you talk to him?'

'No, I didn't,' said Siobhan. 'I told him I had a partner. And then I stood and watched him. Made sure he left. Made sure he was genuine.'

'Would have been kind of cool, wouldn't it? Have a guy come over.'

'What have you managed to do?' asked Siobhan.

'I've found some individuals who are in the industry now. They've all gone up through that route. All unfortunate kids, helped by the Foundation, and back in Derry.'

'You got addresses? Contacts?'

'I'm working on it. We'll have some of them.'

88

'Will you get them sorted? Once you have it, we're on the move.'

'Are you all right?' asked Kylie.

'I'm not sure,' she said, 'really not sure, but get me those addresses. That's our next course of action.'

Siobhan stood and packed her small bag while Kylie fought with the internet to come up with addresses. When Kylie had packed her own bags, the two women headed downstairs for a taxi and a flight back to Northern Ireland.

Kylie and she had been so pumped up flying over. But one night with the team, and Julian, and a chance encounter with a man who just wanted to get to know her, had left her reeling in her head. She'd need to focus though; she'd need to focus. And make sure she didn't get blindsided by anything in the days ahead.

Chapter 12

'Manfred, Manfred, Manfred' said Declan repeatedly as Julian drove the car. When they arrived back in Northern Ireland, they came to find out more about the mysterious Manfred. Julian could have picked up Siobhan's line of enquiry but, having had the women clocked by them and almost taken out, Julian decided a different approach was necessary.

He told Declan he would look up some contacts and see if he could find the name Manfred anywhere. One such person he knew owed Julian a great deal. He had saved his life back in the day and the man, not exactly grateful, knew that he owed Julian a reluctant debt. Julian called him because he was in the police force, and he would know about Manfred if the police knew about him.

It took half a day before the contact came back and asked Julian to meet him at a local beach. Julian advised Declan that he wouldn't be coming to the meeting because the man wouldn't trust Julian if he had somebody else with him. So Declan was allowed to drive, dropping Julian off at the top of the beach.

The day was overcast, despite it being summer, and Julian

walked casually along in his trousers and shirt, with a loose waterproof jacket around him. He could see the man at the far end of the beach, standing with a fishing rod, which was whipped back out into the lough. Julian came up close behind him, before he acknowledged him.

'The fishing good here?'

'No, there's about as much chance of the fish disturbing us as there is someone else. I'd say it's good to see you. But, well, it isn't.'

'The feeling's pretty mutual,' said Julian. 'However, I need you. Did you find out any information?'

'Why are you interested?' asked the man suddenly. 'Why Manfred?'

'He's come up in a case we're investigating. I take it you know that we're now operating on our own? I'm working with Siobhan Duffy out of Gold Coast Investigations.'

'I heard you were operating on Siobhan Duffy,' said the man.

'There's no need to be coarse. She's the boss,' said Julian, 'and the boss wants me to find out about Manfred. That's why I'm here, not to discuss her looks and curves, and how they've changed over the years.'

'No small talk then,' said the man. He had a fishing hat on, as well as waterproof leggings and jacket. There was a seat beside him, along with a large net, and a cool box was also located nearby, presumably to keep fish in when he caught them. Julian wondered if there was a gun in there instead. The cover was excellent and probably important.

'Manfred,' said Julian.

'I heard you had a bit of trouble. Office is closed.'

'It is. Just for a moment. Until things settle down.'

'Settle down? Has it got that rough already? You were never

a guy to make things get rough. Remember back in the day. We were smooth. Nothing in the daylight. Nothing came out. Nothing that would panic people. You had a genuine desire for that. Keep it all below the surface. Things are above the surface with this one.'

'What about Manfred?' asked Julian.

'Well, several food firms have been used by the man for their vehicles. They've done some research and his name's been mentioned here, there, and wherever. Nobody knows who he is; nobody knows exactly what he does, but he's on the intelligence briefings. The food firms in question all seem normal. Above board, legit.'

Julian wondered if he should mention the flat in town, the one that had been owned by Alex Samuels. Maybe the police would know about it too. Maybe they would have known the man that was inside it. But not yet. After all, this was about the client's brother. He didn't want too much attention drawn.

'What sort of food firms?'

'Here, there, wherever. All over the province.'

'Anything in there around Belfast?'

'Shirley's Pastries,' said the man. 'You need to be aware of that. They were observed, and the name mentioned around them, but there's nothing proven.'

Julian looked down into the water.

'What are you doing here?' the man said. 'Why are you here?'

'Honestly? I'm here for her.'

'Most people in your line of work don't stay after their work's done, let alone look for more. She's putting you at risk being here in the long run. Don't you know that? If things kicked off again. Things took a turn for the worse. This isn't a place that forgives and forgets.'

'Oh, I think she'd be aware of that. I don't think she'd stay if that was the case.'

'You have your boy run you down.'

'Yes I did. I thought you'd be watching. I also thought you'd be perturbed if I brought him here.'

'He's your gardener, isn't he?'

'We are picking up a lot of attention,' said Julian. 'Why?'

'Why? Look at what she's been involved in since she got back. We'd just like to know that what she's doing is wholesome. In the public interest.'

'The Service has been speaking to you then. They weren't happy. But then again, they were a mess.'

'Not just the Service watching you. People here. Things are a lot better than they used to be. We want them kept a lot better. We don't want things blowing up.'

'Good pun.'

'I'm not being funny. She needs to keep her oar out of things. People are worried she might go digging in the wrong places. Stir things up. Cause some bad blood.'

'She won't,' said Julian. 'If I have my way, she won't be going back into any of it.'

'If you have your way. She's one of those modern women, though, isn't she? One to decide everything for herself. We're not back in the old, old days when the man ruled the roost, and the woman did what she was told.'

'I was never really like that,' said Julian.'

'You need to have a word with her.'

'Do I? She's the boss. You could have a word with her. You could explain it.'

The man pulled his empty line back out of the water and

then cast it back out into the lough.

'There'll come a time when things will get messy. Maybe not in what you're looking at now, but at some point it will. Other people will get involved. Both of you got through troubled times. Both of you are at an age where you can call it a day. Take my advice and call it a day.'

I want to, thought Julian. *But Siobhan, Siobhan—she'll have to call it a day.*

'As I said, I'm not here to discuss the boss. I'm here to discuss what you know.'

'That's all that I know,' said the man. 'Shirley's Pastries. It's the only one near Belfast. If you do find Manfred, remember where the tip came from. Remember to drop off some intel as a repayment.'

'This is your repayment to me,' said Julian. 'I still remember what we lost.'

'You still blame me for it, don't you?' said the man.

'Completely. Because it was your fault.'

'Mistakes were made. Lots of mistakes. All through those years. Yet you hold this one like a grudge to me.'

'I hold this one as a bargaining chip to find out information. I don't do grudges,' said Julian. 'I don't do all of that. That's why I'm so good.'

Julian turned and began walking back down the beach.

'I hope she's worth it,' the man said after him. 'She pulls you into this mess. I hope she's worth it.'

Julian ignored him, but looked down in towards the lough as he walked. The place was beautiful, truly beautiful. The calmness of the water today, even with the overcast sky. His feet slipped through the soft sand. He'd have to knock out his shoes when he got back up to the road, but Julian didn't care.

He stopped at the end of the beach, knowing that Declan would take another ten minutes before he would pass by again. He didn't want him staying close. It wasn't that sort of meeting. Sitting on a rock, Julian stared at the water. She was worth it, but she had the house. She had a garden looking out, but she needed to take up painting. She needed to do bowls or have afternoons out with coffee. She needed to say goodbye to all of this.

Could he force her to? Could he turn round and tell her she was being an idiot? Would she listen? He knew she valued his opinion, but what ran through Siobhan was stronger than opinion.

At the end of the day, both of them were adults. They knew what they were getting themselves into. Could see things coming. They could avoid things. Declan and Kylie, not so. As much as Siobhan kept pushing how they were growing in the business, how they were getting better at what they did, they didn't make up for the years of training, the years of experience. If they weren't careful, they'd get those two killed. That's why he needed her to come out. Because she wasn't prepared to work on her own. She could kill those kids. Especially taking on clients like this.

He had hoped when she got the business that she'd go for something a little less involved. But as soon as it came through the door, she bit. She bit big time. Because it was what she wanted. The hard stuff. Intoxicating, charging around, all of it. That's what Siobhan wanted. And if Siobhan wanted it, maybe she'd get it. He had to admit, where she was involved, his judgement lacked. *No,* he thought, *his judgment didn't lack. The conviction to walk away from her did.*

You have to walk away from her to make her see you as

95

serious. But he knew it was something he'd never do.

Chapter 13

Armed with his knowledge about Shirley's Pastries' vans, Julian returned back to the house with Declan. On the way, he decided to do a quick check past the offices in Donaghadee. As he drove past, he was disturbed to find a Shirley's Pastries van sitting outside the offices, maybe fifty yards down from the premises.

'Isn't that the people you were talking about?' asked Declan. 'The one your contact said.'

'That's right. Go down and take a right and then drop me off,' said Julian. 'I want to see what they're doing.'

'What do you want me to do?'

'Don't swing past him again. Instead, park up a couple of streets away. Wait for me.'

'Wait for you? Can I come down and see what's going on too?'

'One, Declan, I want to get close. Two, I need somebody ready in case we have to get out of here.'

'Okay,' said Declan. 'You're the boss.'

Julian didn't need a quick getaway car. He wasn't intending on being caught at all. It sounded better for Declan to be an active part of the solution rather than just a slight inconvenience.

Declan pulled the car over and Julian jumped out, well out of sight of the van. He casually pulled his jacket coat up around him and walked around the block on the opposite side to their offices so he would approach the van from behind. He wandered a little way down from it, looking to see if anyone was hovering around the van, maybe being a lookout for them.

When he was sure that there was no one beyond the van, he walked slowly up towards it, with his head looking out towards the sea. He could see the harbour, the split walls, one sitting on its own in the water, the other attached to the land. There were a few ships on the go at the moment. And up ahead, where there used to be the paddling pools everyone played in, everything was quiet because of the overcast sky.

Dandering up beside the van, Julian pulled out his phone, and looked into it, intently pressing buttons. He glanced to his right as he went past the van and saw that the driver was looking over at the offices. Julian walked past, then turned and photographed him through the windscreen. He then walked on, taking photographs out to the harbour and beyond.

Or so he wanted it to look like. He'd also clocked a photograph of the registration of the van before turning back up the street he'd been dropped off in. He found Declan a few streets away in the car.

'What are we up to now, then?' asked Declan.

'We'll take the car, we'll come up behind them, we'll park up, and we'll wait and see if they leave.'

'You don't want to, like, disturb them or pop into the office to see if they'll come in,' said Declan.

'No, I don't,' said Julian. 'They're unaware of us. I want them to stay unaware of what we're doing. If we're lucky, they're going to tell us everything as if I was speaking to them.'

Declan looked at him, slightly bemused. That made Julian smile.

'So, you're thinking we follow them, and they show us where they live, what they do with the van, stuff like that?'

'Exactly,' said Julian. 'One of the key things when you're investigating is make sure that people don't know you're investigating. They'll tell you more or show you more if they don't know what you're looking at or if you're after them.'

'Right,' said Julian. He parked the car up some distance down and they sat for the next two hours while the van didn't move. When it did, Declan pulled out behind it.

'Keep your distance,' said Julian. 'Keep your distance. We've got two sets of eyes in this car. You can watch the road; I can watch them. Tell you where they went. You just keep yourself safe on the road. Don't have an accident. It tends to draw attention.'

Julian saw Declan's focused face and almost laughed. But it reminded him he wasn't on the same level as Siobhan and Julian. The qualms about what he was leading them into came back to him again.

The van returned to Belfast, and it was now late evening. They pulled up outside the Shirley's Pastries' factory. Julian got Declan to park around the corner. He jumped out, holding his binoculars in his hand, and went to the street corner to peer around. Declan got out behind him quietly. However, Julian heard him.

'We will not look good on a street corner together,' said Julian, 'back to the car, please.'

'I just thought I could.'

'Back to the car, please,' said Julian. 'If they're on the move again, I'll want the car up beside me in an instant.'

Declan hurried off, and Julian saw the man who was driving the van get out, and then go with a colleague to get into a car in the firm's car park. The blue estate pulled out as Julian waved for Declan to roll up in the car beside him.

He jumped in and followed the blue car off into the depths of Belfast. The man first pulled up at an estate that looked not run down, but certainly one of the lower end in terms of quality of house build. It was older than most, and when the man stepped out, Declan asked, 'Do you want to stay? I'll follow him.'

'No. He's not the guy who was in the van.'

'Okay,' said Declan and he continued following the car with the man from the van. It disappeared off into the heart of the city and was parked before a set of flats. These were not as salubrious as the ones Alex lived in. But they certainly cost a reasonable packet.

'Wow, look at those.'

'Pull over,' said Julian. He jumped out, indicated to Declan to keep driving round, and disappeared to the corner of the flats. He saw the man press a buzzer. The door opened. Julian took a chance, quickly coming up behind him and got his foot in the door before it closed.

He stepped inside, now only a few feet behind the man. Julian turned quickly over towards where there were letter boxes for each of the flats. He reached out and fiddled with one, his back to the man, and heard the man climbing stairs. Once he'd spent a minute there and knew the man was up at least two flights of stairs, Julian followed him.

He was cautious, keeping his face away from cameras. Inside the building, the man climbed three floors and Julian saw him go to a flat, open the door, and step inside. Julian approached, looking at the name on it. Morrison. Of course, that meant nothing. Maybe this was Manfred. Maybe it was one of his goons. Maybe it had nothing to do with Manfred.

Somebody else was maybe after them. Everything was just too mixed up at the moment. He didn't know what was going on, didn't know who was involved. He was not happy with the way things were panning out. So, he needed to get a grip of this. Julian made his way back down out of the flat and walked another way away from the building before sticking his thumb out as Declan passed. He jumped into the car.

'So,' said Declan, 'what do we know then?'

'We know he's wanting to watch us. We know he earns a lot more money than we do, working at Shirley's pastries. We're going to watch this man, Declan, and you're going to take the first shift.' Declan's face looked eager.

'Where do I do it from?' he said.

'You're going to park up in the multi-storey car park over there and you're going to watch, sitting in the car.'

'OK,' said Julian. 'What are you going to do?'

'Sleep. We're not going back to the house. We're going to go from here. Shall I get you some food before we start?'

'So what? We just stand in the car park waiting for him to come out. One of us asleep, one of us awake.'

'I'm out of a job, Declan,' said Julian. 'No other way to do it. I don't know where he goes. I know where he possibly lives. But he hasn't come back here a second time yet. For all I know, somebody else lives in that flat and he's staying with him for a moment. Nope. We need to follow him. Whoever Morrison is.'

'OK,' said Declan, 'but you've got to get me a burger.'

'You really need to eat properly,' said Julian, 'it affects what you do.'

'What would you suggest?'

Julian wanted some chicken and rice. Not because it would help him, but because that's what he liked to eat. Still, as long as Declan thought it was good for him, it probably would be better than a burger.

Chapter 14

Siobhan and Kylie flew into Belfast, picking up her car before driving it out of the city towards Armagh. Kylie had identified several young actors and actresses who were now located out there on tour. A local theatre was running a play for a couple of nights and it seemed several of those who had gone through Randolph's fund were now working together there. Maybe that was the case. Maybe they got noticed by the same people. But it worked for Siobhan because they weren't travelling all over the country to interview different people. She arrived at the theatre to find rehearsals underway and spoke to one of the proprietors.

'I really could do with talking to some of your actors and actresses in there,' said Siobhan. 'It's a matter of urgency.'

'Something serious?' asked the man.

'Well, not that serious,' said Siobhan. 'But—'

'You'll have to wait, then. It'll be about another hour before rehearsals are done. Then they'll be having their break. I suggest you catch them then.'

Siobhan took Kylie for a coffee, and after a chicken roll, came back ready to interview their actors. The proprietor took them backstage and into the changing rooms once he'd made sure that everyone was decent.

'Hello everyone,' said Siobhan when she was brought in. 'My name is Siobhan Duffy. I'm from Gold Coast Investigations. This is to do with background on a case I'm involved in, just some information I'm looking for. I believe several of you went through Randolph Frederick's fund out of Derry.'

'That's right,' said one of the girls. 'Mary and I went through that. So did Connor and Eamon. Emily did as well.'

'I was just wondering how you found it.'

A young lad from the side spoke in. 'I'm Connor. It's made me. It's given me this job.'

'And what was it like?'

'Well, we got a lot of funding at the time. People came back to the hall we were at in Derry. Helped train us there. Got us into the local theatre for a bit of work. But they also took us away to one of his estates. That was the best. You had some of the top actors. You're not allowed to mention who they were, though. They don't want to be seen to be doing something like that. They said it wasn't for their agent, because if they got hold of it, they'd be telling everyone.'

'That's right,' said another male voice. 'I'm Eamon. It was quite fantastic. I don't think I'd be here now without it. I think, in fact, I'd probably not have a job at all. They sought us out around the area if they thought you had talent, and I had little talent. But they brought it on, and developed it, and now here I am. It strikes me just how fortunate I am.'

'How about you, Mary?' asked Siobhan. 'How did you find it?'

'Very similar. It's just terrific to have somebody who can teach you all the basics and then more. And then go further.'

'What about when you went away?'

'Well, that was a bit scary, because at the time,' said Mary, 'I wasn't that old. We were all together, though. That was the good side of it. We had these professional actors come in and they pushed you. Oh, they pushed you, but we had the best of accommodation. They had little parties and stuff for us. We were treated really, really well.'

'Were your families with you?'

'No, we went away with actors. It was good getting away from the family, though. None of that pressure. You were just there to learn. Families put competitive elements in, don't they?' said Mary.

'Too right,' said Eamon. 'My family wanted me to be better than him, better than her. Wanted me to be better than Connor here because we'd be going for the same jobs. Well, I wouldn't have that. We're good friends now and we're working together.'

'So, you would say that your time was good?'

'Time was better than good,' said Eamon. 'Time was terrific.'

'How many others do you know went through the program?'

'Not many. They only took five or six at a time,' said Mary. 'Emily did it, too. She's not here at the moment.'

'So overall,' said Kylie, 'you're giving it a big thumbs up.'

'Most of us wouldn't be here without it. Sad when he died.'

'You met him?' asked Siobhan.

'Oh yeah—I mean he wasn't there the whole time; most of the time we were with actors. We were learning what we were doing. That was the whole point of it after all, but we saw him. A nice man, a delightful man.'

'Total gent,' said Conor.

'If you don't mind,' said Maria, 'maybe we could go and get some lunch.'

'Of course,' said Siobhan. She let them disappear from the changing room and turned to Kylie. 'What do you think?'

'They play their part well, don't they,' said Kylie.

'How do you mean?'

'Well, we've just talked to a bunch of actors and I think they've been acting. It was all so bland, so wonderful the whole time, not a hilarious moment, not a slight mishap or one downside to it. Everything was wonderful,'

'You're getting better at this, aren't you?' said Siobhan. 'That's what I thought.'

Suddenly, another girl came into the room, and she looked at them quizzically.

'Apologies, I'm Siobhan Duffy, this is Kylie. We've just been in asking some of the actors some questions.'

'Wonderful. I'm one of the actors,' the girl said. 'Emily.'

'Oh,' said Kylie. 'You were at Randolph Frederick's lessons? The fund coming out of Derry.'

'I was.' Emily was blonde-haired with a small frame and stature but she gave a smile, showing perfect, white teeth.

'Do you mind if we ask you some questions about it?'

'Who are you again?'

'Siobhan Duffy. Gold Coast Investigations. We're just trying to get some background for a case we're on.'

'Well, if you want.'

'Your friends said that it was a really positive experience for them. Is that the same for you?'

'Well, yes. I'm here. I've done well. Everything's gone superbly.'

Siobhan looked at the girl's face. It looked very down, not matching the ringing endorsement coming from her lips.

'But what?' asked Siobhan.

'Well, you see, I've got a friend, Emma. Emma was quite stunning. Very attractive. I got here because of my talent,' said Emily. 'That didn't happen for Emma. Don't get me wrong. She could act a bit, but she didn't have what the rest of us had. What she had was looks.'

'And what happened to Emma?' asked Siobhan.

'Look, you need to keep this quiet. This didn't come from me, okay? We have to talk properly and nicely about our experiences. And that's not difficult because my experience was a good one. Emma's wasn't. So, you need to keep it quiet. If they found out I'm telling you this, I'd probably lose the job. I'd probably lose my income. It's hard enough getting acting roles.'

'You have my word,' said Siobhan.

'Emma's—well, she's living on the edge of Belfast now. And she's tied into some terrible people. It all came because she got into a lot of trouble.'

'What do you mean?'

'Well, Emma wasn't always with us. Men take a shine to Emma because of the way she looks, the way she is. She was quite flirty back in the day as well. The kind of girl that liked to be the centre of attention. It's all right, but sometimes the attention isn't good, is it?'

'You think she's turned to bad people now? What sort of bad people?' asked Kylie.

'I don't ask. I don't want to get involved with that. Okay? I've told you too much already.'

'You think you can get me an address?' asked Siobhan.

'Give me your phone,' said the girl. She took it, tapped in an address, and handed it back to Siobhan.

'Can you remember that?' asked the woman.

'Yes,' said Siobhan.

'Then wipe it. So, it's not even on your phone.'

'Okay. I'll be needing to get on. All right. I'm going to be seeing the others for lunch. The fact I've stopped with you won't be suspicious, but if I stay too long, they'll think I'm telling you more than the script.'

'But it's not a script for you,' said Kylie. 'You did okay.'

'I think that's what they do. Some of us are okay. Some of the others, well . . . Emma will have to tell you. She never told me everything. She knows what it's about. I need to go.' Emily turned and walked out of the door, closing it hard behind her.

'What do you think about that?' asked Kylie.

'Leave the building first,' said Siobhan. She opened the door to find the proprietor outside. She thanked him. He escorted her out of the building, along with Kylie. They returned to the car and sat down.

'I'll ask again then,' said Kylie. 'What did you think of that?'

'Do you trust her?'

'Well, she seemed genuine,' said Kylie.

'But, like you said, we're with a load of actors. If they can't act, if they can't sell you the story, who can?'

'But the rest didn't, did they? They'd have known. Emma?' said Kylie. 'Maybe she was just close to her friends. Maybe.'

'Yeah, maybe,' said Siobhan.

'Do you want to look for some others, then? Get more stories?'

'No. I doubt it,' said Siobhan. 'I think there we'll get the same story. Emily's told us something different. We need to check it out. We've got an address. So let's talk to the woman.'

Kylie started the car, and they pulled away leaving Armagh to head for Belfast. As they drove, Siobhan turned to Kylie in the driver's seat.

'What do you think I'm like?'

'I'm sorry?'

'You think I just charge in? You think I can't be persuaded off something?'

'Well?' said Kylie.

'No. Don't think about it. Say the first thing. Say what you really think.'

'You're my boss. What do you want me to do? Tell you that? You'd probably sack me.'

Siobhan sat back for a moment. 'It's really that bad an opinion?'

'It's not that bad an opinion. It's just that some of your strengths you might see as weaknesses or as not conducive to your work.'

'My ways are conducive to my work. It's what keeps me together, it's what keeps me—'

'It's what gets you into trouble,' said Kylie. 'Is this about Julian? Is this Julian telling you to back off, saying that we should have been out of this case?'

'Kind of,' said Siobhan, 'why?'

'I'm just aware that you've jumped in with me and Declan. We both said we should keep investigating. I'm not so sure anymore.'

'Why?'

'Because, it's the thing about Julian. He's clever, cleverer than you in a lot of ways.' Siobhan raised an eyebrow. 'Oh, don't take it like that. He's not as invested. Well, he's invested in you. He's not invested in the business. In fact, I think he might be a bit disappointed that this is what you're doing.'

'What do you mean?'

'He's indulging you, how Declan indulges me. If he thinks I like to do something, he comes along and does it, even if he hates it. It's the price men pay, isn't it?'

'But Julian wouldn't.'

'Julian gave up the Service for you. Julian would never have given up the Service,' said Kylie. 'Now he's part of your team. He's playing second fiddle to someone in an investigation agency, after being one of the top men in the service. You're telling me he's not doing it for you?'

'Okay. So he's telling me he's not doing it for me. So what should I do?'

'You're asking me, after telling me how wise you are, how much older you've been. All this time I've known you, and now you're asking me?'

'I don't seem to have got a hold of him at all, really understood him.'

'Well, we don't, do we? You need to decide what you want. Do you want to keep charging around, or do you want Julian?'

'You think he won't stay?'

'He'll definitely stay. He'll always stay with you. You'll make him your lackey. your puppy dog beside you. He'll be your lackey. You want Julian the wolf.'

'You see him as a wolf,' said Siobhan.

'In investigation terms, yes,' said Kylie. 'He's a wolf. You're a lioness. You're determined, you're so focused. But he doesn't want this anymore. I think he wants out. I think he just wants you. But he's going to take you whatever way you are going to be. Maybe you need to meet him at some halfway point. At least you need to talk to him.'

Siobhan sat back in the seat. It wasn't the answer she'd been expecting. She was expecting confirmation that she'd been right, and the investigation was important. She looked out of the window at the countryside rolling past. *Hmm*, she thought. *Missing the wolf. Could Julian do without this type of work in his life? Could she?* Siobhan wondered.

Chapter 15

Y ou stay in the car,' Siobhan said to Kylie. 'I don't know what we're going to face when we get to the address. She might be on her own; she might be with other people. I might need to beat a hasty retreat. Always a good bet to have somebody in the car waiting.'

'You sure you don't want me with you? I mean, I could give you some assistance.'

'In what way?' asked Siobhan. 'Tell me exactly how you're going to assist me. It won't be physically. I can handle myself. You will add nothing to the mix. And I know what questions I want to ask her.'

'Well, thanks for bursting my bubble,' said Kylie. 'I'll sit in the car then.'

'It wasn't meant like that. You've got to be careful. You were the one telling me what Julian says. Is Julian right? Well, I'm trying to make judgement calls on the possible dangers.'

'Whatever,' said Kylie.

Siobhan wrapped her coat around her, because, although it was summer, it was a dark evening with sinister grey clouds reflected overhead. It was around eleven o'clock at night. Siobhan thought she would catch the woman in. If she'd gone to bed, well, then she'd be desperate to get rid of Siobhan quickly. And she might be more forthcoming with information. The estate she lived on wasn't a bad one. Most people here were normal, everyday folk, probably towards the lower rung of society, in terms of finance. Otherwise, salt of the earth, as her mother would have said.

She walked up the small driveway to the semi-detached house, looked for a bell, and then rapped on the door. She could hear a shout from inside, a kind of grump, and then someone switched on the hallway light. The door opened five seconds later to reveal a woman in a dressing gown.

She had blonde hair; her eyes were full of bags. Siobhan looked and wondered if she'd slept well; if she hadn't done whatever she'd done to her body, would this woman be good looking? Would this be a someone who would attract? She reckoned she would have been.

'Yeah?' said the woman.

'I'm Siobhan Duffy with Gold Coast Investigations. I'm looking to speak to Emma.'

'Well, you're looking at her. What the hell do you want?'

'I want to talk about Randolph Frederick and his fund.'

'Why? What the hell do you want to talk to me about that for? You think I've got anything to say?'

'Well, do you?' asked Siobhan. 'Someone told me you didn't have the greatest of experience with him.'

'I don't talk to anyone, all right?'

'Absolutely no one?'

'Well, you can clear off.'

There's a shout from inside. 'Who's that, Em? Who's that?'

'No one. Be on their way in a minute.'

'Is that your boyfriend?'

The woman's eyes flicked away for a moment. 'You could call him that. He's a nasty piece of work. You really don't want to be dealing with him.'

'I'm all right,' said Siobhan 'I can handle myself. Tell me. Tell me about Frederick's fund. You went for the training with him. I got told that different things happened to you.'

'Nothing happened to me,' said the woman. She was gazing off to the side. 'Nothing, all right? Whoever told you that, they're a damn liar. Now away and catch yourself on. Get the hell out of here. I'm telling you, if he comes out to the door, I don't know what he'll do.'

'He can do whatever the hell he wants,' said Siobhan. 'I want to know your story. I want a—'

'I don't want to bloody well tell you, okay? Why should I? All it's going to do is get me grief.'

'I'll come in for a minute,' said Siobhan. 'Why don't I do that?'

'That's not wise,' said the woman. 'He'll know you're inside.'

'And if he comes to me, he'll get what for.'

'You don't understand,' said Emma, slightly panicked. 'He's not to be trifled with. He's as likely to pull a gun on you as anything else.'

'I've dealt with guns before.'

Siobhan could sense that there was an impasse coming and wasn't sure quite what to do. Kylie was still back in the car, but if she'd turned and walked away, she wouldn't have got anything. Could she watch this girl with a violent man looking after her? Was he involved? She didn't know. She thought she should force the issue.

'I think I should come in,' said Siobhan. The girl put two hands up in front of her.

'No, don't.' Siobhan stepped through.

'I told you not to bloody well come in. He'll get up in a minute. He's going to come through. Do you realise that? What do you think he's going to do?'

'I don't care what he's going to do. Clearly, something happened. Clearly, Randolph's fund wasn't the best thing for you. Somebody told me you were a beauty in your day. You don't look that way now.'

The girl turned her head to one side. Siobhan could see a bruise across the side of her face, running down her cheekbone.

'What the hell's that?' asked Siobhan. 'Did he do that?'

'I fell, all right?' said Emma.

'What the blazes is going on out there? Is that person giving you problems? I might have to get up off this couch. There'll be hell to pay.'

'Tell him to stay on the couch,' whispered Siobhan. 'Just let him stay there. You can talk to me. You can tell me what they did.'

'Are you some sort of press person?'

'No, I told you. Siobhan Duffy, Gold Coast Investigations. I'm here to help.'

'I don't see how it's going to help me,' said Emma. Siobhan looked down at Emma's arms, now clear of the sleeves of her dressing gown. There were large bruises along them as well.

'Does he beat you?' asked Siobhan.

'Told you. Just go. Not worth it.'

'That's it,' said a voice from inside. 'I'll get rid of them for you, Em. Don't worry. Where the hell are they?'

Siobhan could hear a man standing inside and thump round towards the door. The living room door opened and a man at least six feet tall and as wide as a brick house looked at her.

'Who the hell are you?'

Siobhan stood in her long coat and looked up towards the man. 'Siobhan Duffy, Gold Coast Investigations. I'm talking to Emma.'

'Don't want you to talk to Emma.'

'I'm not bothered about what you want,' said Siobhan. 'I should give you a good beating, seeing what you've done to her.'

'You want to make something of it?' said the man. 'She gave lip. That's what happened to her. It'll happen to you.'

'You a finger on me and I'll break your jaw,' said Siobhan.

'With what?' he said.

'I don't need much. Don't worry about that.' She turned back to Emma. 'Ignore him. Tell me. Frederick's fund. What did they do to you?'

'You shut your mouth, Emma,' said the man. 'And you, get the hell out of this house. You can piss right off.'

'I don't like your tone,' said Siobhan. 'I really don't like your tone. Get back inside and watch your telly.'

She turned back to Emma again. 'Emma, I really can help.'

Siobhan saw the man step forward. As soon as he put his first foot forward, she reacted by raising her booted foot. Although she had a short heel, she used it to great effect, slamming it down onto the toes at the front of his foot. He yelled, and she stepped forward, driving two fingers into his throat.

He fell backwards, banging his head off the wall. She could hear him gasping for breath.

'I'll ask you again, Emma. What did Fredericks do to you? All the people that were with you—they're enjoying wonderful careers. You haven't. Is that because you looked good?'

'No.'

"The others just not his type. Were they? Or did you just not scream?'

'I don't want to talk about it,' she said. 'Go away.'

'She's right,' said the man. 'You can fuck off.'

'I don't like that language,' said Siobhan. 'I really don't like that language. I'm having a civil conversation with my friend here. You lie there and shut up.'

The man was getting back up, though, and Siobhan realised he probably would not go away. He stepped forward, and Siobhan stood to the side before stamping hard once again onto his foot with her heel.

'Why, you bitch!' he yelled. He swung a right hand, and Siobhan pushed Emma to one side. She leaned back to the other side, the fist flying past her face. She jabbed him hard in the stomach, and then with her other hand, grabbed his ear, twisting it as brutally as she could, almost to the point of it ripping off.

'I told you, get the hell out of here. Let me talk.' She kicked hard into the back of his leg, forcing him down on his knees, and then kicked him in the back, making him fall to the floor. He dragged himself forward into the living room as Siobhan turned back to Emma.

'I'm not afraid of anyone,' said Siobhan. 'I can help. I'm used to dealing with people like that.'

'Don't,' she said. 'Don't.' The woman stepped forward, and quietly whispered in Siobhan's ear, 'Tomorrow, midday. Zanoo's.'

Zanoo's was a ladies' clothes shop, a little more modern than Siobhan liked. She knew where it was, but she retorted, 'You can come now if you want, I'll take you away from him.'

117

The woman shook her head. Siobhan heard the shuffle of a drawer followed by a slam in the living room. She stepped to one side of the living room door, as the man marched through, gun held in front of him. Siobhan caught his wrist, twisted it sharply, and the gun fell to the floor. She kicked it down the hall. Once again, she drove two fingers up into his throat, making him gurgle, then pushed him back, making him stumble to the floor.

'You leave her alone tonight,' Siobhan said to him. 'If you don't, I'll come back for you. I'll do a proper job. Ever pull a gun on me again, and it'll be the last gun you pull.'

She nodded at the woman for a moment, and then said, 'Are you sure you won't talk?'

'No,' said the woman, shaking her head.

Siobhan turned and walked out of the house, down the driveway. She was shaking inside. The guy was big, and she had to be quick and get there first with him. Then he'd come with the gun. She'd guessed everything correctly, seen what would happen, and dealt with it. But even so, Siobhan felt queasy as she got into the car beside Kylie.

'Get us to a hotel for the night.'

'Did it not go well?' asked Kylie.

'It went very well. We've got a meeting tomorrow. But they weren't wrong when they said she got into bad company. Guy in there was nasty. I just don't know how nasty yet.'

Siobhan looked at her hands and could see blood on her nails. She'd obviously driven them in sharply. He wouldn't forget her. That wasn't always a good thing. Sometimes that made them react quicker to you. Not ask questions, not stop you. Just hit you before you even saw them.

But that girl was in there. Emma was trapped. So she'd meet

tomorrow, and she'd encourage her to come with her. Take her away from the situation.

'You all right?' asked Kylie, as the car drove off. 'You seem very—'

'I'm fine,' said Siobhan. 'A lot on my mind, Kylie. That's all. A lot on my mind.'

Chapter 16

'Y ou look ready to drop,' said Julian. It was mid-morning, and they had been sleeping in four-hour shifts. Declan looked exhausted.

'I don't know how you sleep in the car,' said Declan. 'I think I'm too big for it.'

'Take the day,' said Julian. 'Go home and get some sleep. Go to the hotel. Crash out,'

'Not back to Siobhan's.'

'No,' said Julian. 'I think with being watched, we keep away from our normal haunts. Just find a room, sleep for the day, and call me when you're up. You can take the first night shift.'

'Are you sure? I mean, you're not going to be able to eat or whatever.'

'He'll be out of there in the next four or five hours, at most. A man like that doesn't stay in all day.'

Declan nodded, and Julian took the binoculars, watching closely. He'd have to run for the car if the man went off in his car, or grabbed a taxi, but Declan was shattered.

It was two hours before there was movement in the flat. Julian watched him closely through a window without curtains. He didn't seem to have picked up any car keys, so Julian made the choice to go down to the street and follow him. By the time the man exited the building, Julian was there, in position.

He felt rough, though. As he hadn't had a shower, he probably smelled bad. He'd eaten some sort of junk food through the night that Declan had come back with, but at least he'd slept, unlike Declan.

The man caught a bus into town, and he had a bag with him. It was a black duffel, and Julian watched it closely. He kept it near him, always being careful with it. When he stepped off into the middle of town, Julian followed and saw him go into a gym.

Julian made his way into the cafe of the gym and could watch the man working out inside. Morrison, if indeed that was his name, seemed to be uninhibited, working away, pumping iron left, right, and centre. Julian watched him spying some other people bench pressing. He saw Morrison had a roving eye over certain women, but he seemed to be no different from any other gym monkey.

Julian texted Siobhan to say what he was doing. Julian got a message in return. She was going to meet someone. Rather than meet up to communicate, in case one was being followed, they kept the messages short and simple, through texts.

The man left the gym, after what Julian presumed must have been a shower, and made his way to Belfast Library. He sat down, read some papers, and picked a few books up off the shelves.

Julian couldn't work out just what he was doing. One of the books he picked up was about weightlifting. He seemed to read that for the longest. Then, with a sudden snap, the book was closed. He took it back to the shelf and left the building.

It was now just after eleven o'clock, and Julian wondered

where he would go next. Morrison stopped at a little cafe. It was cramped, and Julian decided against sitting inside it with him. There were maybe five tables, a city centre cafe. It probably wouldn't be there in a year's time.

Julian stepped into the music shop across the road. He stood glancing through music books in front of him, but his eye was across the road watching the man. He was drinking coffee as far as Julian could tell, and then a woman entered the coffee shop. She sat down.

The woman seemed very animated, talking, while Morrison sat there. She had considerable volume given her animation and the size of her mouth as it opened and closed. Finally, Julian decided that she probably wasn't telling Morrison anything of importance.

She was dressed in an alluring fashion, not overtly, but clearly she'd spent a bit of time trying to look her best for meeting him. It may have been a cover, of course, to give the impression that this was boyfriend and girlfriend, or a man with his partner. Julian couldn't decide what was going on. At one point, they reached across the table, hands touching, but Julian saw nothing that would make him feel uneasy.

'Any of the music to your fancy, sir?'

Julian turned his head to see one of the store assistants talking to him.

'Saxophone,' he said. 'I'm learning saxophone. Would you have anything for a beginner? Some of these pieces look too hard.'

The man looked down. 'Are you able to transcribe?'

'No, I need to have it in E flat, thanks.'

'Very good,' said the man.

He started flicking through some of the music books in front of Julian. But Julian's eyes were across the road. Once again, the couple were animated. The woman, especially so. But again, it looked all for show.

'I have this. You look like a man from the eighties. Maybe a bit of Curtis Stigers? These are quite simple arrangements. Something you could get on with while enjoying it.'

'Well, that sounds excellent. Anything else?' asked Julian. He didn't turn once to face the man, his eyes never leaving the cafe.

'Well, I'll have a look, sir.'

Julian ignored the man as his fingers sped over the different music books. They'd been in there ten minutes, and they were looking like they were about to go.

They aren't a couple, thought Julian. He also didn't like people that rushed their coffee, but he tried to ignore this and keep in mind that he wasn't here for that.

'Here's another one,' said the man. 'It's some simple arrangements to Billy Joel numbers.'

'Excellent,' said Julian. 'Wrap them up for me, please.'

'But of course,' said the man, 'if you come this way to the till.'

'Just wrap them up for me. I've got my card here. If you could bring the reader over.' Julian kept his eye on the couple. The woman stood up, gave Morrison a kiss on the cheek, and then walked to the front door of the coffee shop. Morrison followed closely behind her. As he did so, Julian saw it; the quick switch. The envelope coming down inside her sleeve, passed back to him, which he then secreted quickly inside his own jacket.

'I really must insist you come over, sir. We do walkabouts.'

Julian walked over. 'How much?' he asked.

'Twenty-five, sir.'

Julian reached inside his pocket, grabbed what he thought was two twenties, and threw them onto the counter.

'Tip for your excellent service,' he said.

Julian reached out, took the books that were now in a paper bag, and walked out of the music store, watching Morrison the whole time. He partly regretted leaving Declan behind, wondering if he could have followed the woman, but it would be too risky. He didn't know what he was doing.

Morrison was the main event, though. He'd been given an envelope and the woman was probably just a runner. Julian walked closely behind him, wondering if the envelope would make an appearance into the bag, but the man didn't go straight home.

Instead, he stopped off in another coffee shop, and Julian walked straight on past. He thought about turning back round, but instead, he made his way inside a sweet shop to stand looking at the papers. As he did so, his eyes caught the woman walking past.

Clever, he thought. She'd gone the other way, then doubled back to see if anyone was following Morrison. Julian took his coat, turned it inside out, and then grabbed a hat from one of his pockets. He slapped it on his head and exited before walking back to the coffee shop the man had gone into.

This time he sat inside, ordering a coffee, but sitting well to the back, away from Morrison. The man's eyes were everywhere. When he was being taught by the service, Julian always remembered his mentor saying, look around but never be seen looking.

It was tough to do, to turn your head naturally. But people did it all the time. They were those people who just watched. That's what they enjoyed in life, going into a cafe, sitting down and watching the world go by, watching all the people. You didn't think they were staring at you. You just thought they were watching.

Julian sipped his coffee. He pulled out his music books and sat looking at them. He'd never played saxophone in his life, but he took out a pen and started marking up original notes on them. Julian saw Morrison looking at him but Julian didn't flinch and continued to mark up.

After a while, the woman he had seen in the first cafe came back. She walked up to the man, whispered something, and then disappeared. She'd done her check; he wasn't being followed. Morrison was clear to go on his way. He stood up and left the coffee house. Julian looked out of the window. Was the woman definitely away?

He'd have to risk it anyway; otherwise, he'd lose Morrison. He stood up, left, still carrying his music, and followed the man back through the streets until he got to his flat again. Julian walked past and retook his position back in the car park.

Julian spent the rest of the afternoon looking down with his stomach grumbling before Declan texted a message. Julian couldn't wait for more food, so he told Declan to get to the car park and to bring him something to eat. When he did so, Julian was disgusted to see it was a burger with cheese, but it would have to do.

'Did you get any further with him?' asked Declan.

'He's received a message. I don't know what it is. I don't know what it's about. There was a woman who came to speak to him. They did it subtly as they left the cafe. She then doubled back, looking for anybody that was watching him. So he's obviously somebody.'

'Is it normal to put all these other things in place?'

'You've got to be good to do stuff like that. To turn round and try to pick up on all the people watching you. When the woman came back, I nearly missed her.'

'Did she see you then?'

'Well, they've both seen me. They just don't know I was watching them. Down there,' said Julian, 'is a couple of music books for the saxophone. I don't suppose you play, do you?'

'No,' said Declan. 'What did you get those for?'

'It's all cover,' he said. 'I had to watch them from a music shop. The coffee shop they were in was too small, too crowded. That shows that they know what they're about again. I told Siobhan we were in with the big boys. The more and more we get into this, the more and more I think I'm right. When are you going to take over, Declan? I could do with a bit of shut eye.'

'I'm ready now, if you want.'

Julian handed the binoculars over. 'I don't think he's going back out today, but we need to be sure.'

Julian made his way back to the car and curled up in the rear seat. The darkened window stopped anybody looking in and he soon fell asleep. He woke up after half an hour, his mind churning.

Thoughts of what was going on ran though his head. Alex bounced about his consciousness. He couldn't fathom it. He couldn't quite grasp it. They seemed to be chasing shadows, and yet nobody was telling them anything about Alex.

It started off with that impossible presumption. Alex was a hitman. Really? Well, the world he was operating in seemed that way, but Julian wasn't so sure he was a hitman. Something just didn't seem right. As for what Fredericks had been up to, who knew?

He lay there, trying to think of Siobhan, but the more he did, the more he saw her as just a stubborn woman who'd never back down. She'd lead him into the grave, he thought. She might lead all of them into the grave. 'So be it,' he said He'd waited his life for her. And if that's where she was going, he'd follow her there, too.

Chapter 17

Siobhan Duffy stood in the store beside Kylie, carefully picking clothes off the rack.

'Think she'll be on time? She's got another, what, two minutes to be here.'

'She said midday, Kylie. She's not going to be spot-on, is she? Especially if she's got someone with her. You've got to give her some leeway here. She might not have been able to get out on time. You don't know what pressure she's under. You don't know what else she's doing, okay? Just chill, Kylie. Goodness' sake!'

'Chill? You just told me to chill. When did you learn to chill? When was that word part of your vocabulary?'

'Let me remind you, this is the boss,' said Siobhan. 'Anyway, what do you think of this top?' Siobhan looked over.

Coyly, Kylie looked at Siobhan. 'I think it's too young for you.'

'Do you prepare all the barbs yourself?' asked Siobhan.

She looked up, and saw Emma entering the shop. Zanoo's was busy, but Emma wasn't difficult to pick out from the crowd, mainly because of the rather large man who came in with her. Siobhan clocked him as the man from the other

128

night and retreated behind a stylish set of dresses.

'He can't see me,' she said to Kylie. 'You're going to have to make contact with her. Tell her where to go. We're going to want her to try on some clothes because he can't go in there. Not with the number of women about. But you'll need to speak to her.'

'How do I do that?'

'See what rail she goes for. Pick something up and drop it. Hopefully, she'll come down to help you. And just say to her, "Siobhan, changing room, now." That's all you have to say. Whisper it. Make sure he doesn't hear.'

'And if he does.'

'Get out quick,' said Siobhan. 'I'll be watching from a distance in case things go very south. But don't let them. We need to talk to this woman.'

Kylie nodded, then disappeared off into the shop. Siobhan watched her from behind the dresses and smiled. Kylie didn't make a beeline for Emma, instead moving subtly around different racks, looking at them.

When Emma made her way into the lingerie section, Kylie followed her in. Siobhan observed the man standing behind her. He had been a thug last night but, like all men, he seemed uncomfortable in the lingerie section. Was it a thing with men that they were worried they were going to get called out, be accused of being some sort of pervert because of where they were standing?

She smiled to herself, for Kylie used the opportunity as the man looked away, lifting a bra off the rack in front of Emma. Kylie leaned in quickly and delivered the message. She then put the bra back and moved along, lifting several others out, popping a few into a basket and then disappearing off with them.

Siobhan then watched Emma, who moved away from the lingerie section to a rack of tops. She picked them up, put them across her and asked her companion whether they fitted. He clearly did not know. So, Emma said she was going to go inside to try them on. The man nodded, said something and then wandered off, presumably to find a men's section. Siobhan swept around with a dress, keeping plenty of clothing between her and the man, before she entered the changing rooms as well.

'Just the one item, ma'am?' asked the woman on the door.

'Yes,' said Siobhan. She walked along the changing room, looking to peer in behind the curtains. Where she couldn't see, she flicked them slightly, until she found Emma. She was changing into a top, and gasped as Siobhan opened the curtains, stepped inside quickly, and enclosed it behind her.

'He's still out there,' she said quickly. 'He hasn't seen me.'

'Who was that with you.'

'My associate. I don't work alone. We haven't got long. You're trying on tops.'

'I can be all day in here and he won't be bothered. It's about the one thing he lets me do, try on clothing.'

'So,' said Siobhan, 'you want to tell me what happened?'

The woman sat down in the chair in the changing room, while Siobhan stood near the curtain. She had it cracked slightly open so she could see who was coming in and out of the changing rooms, worried in case the man should come in, even though he was never meant to. These were women's changing rooms, after all.

'I did go with Frederick's fund. It was great to begin with. Super, in fact. We would simply go along and they had some decent actors to help us. And we got good. But one day, Randolph Fredericks came along. I was all excited. He picked me out as a future star. But then I realised why.'

'What age were you?'

'Sixteen.'

'And he did what?'

'He didn't do anything then. He talked to me a lot. Got close to me. Told me how wonderful I was, but when I look back, his eyes were all over me. He likes the young ones. I found that out later.'

'Did he?'

'When we went to his estate, we got acting lessons, but at night some of us got a special visit. The others didn't know about it until I told some of them. You went to your room about eight because it was a long day of acting. Some phoned home but someone else came for me. Me and a couple of other girls. We were taken to meet Randolph.'

Siobhan could see tears in the woman's eyes. She didn't want her crying. It wouldn't look good when she went back out.

'Try to hold it together,' she said. 'Take the emotion out of it if you can. You don't want to be emotional going back out. He'll realise something's up.'

The woman nodded. 'Simply, we were dressed provocatively. Randolph, well, he did have his way. When it came time to move on and to get given parts, I was asked to go overseas. Everyone thought it was wonderful, except it wasn't. Over in England, that's where it all changed. I got away eventually, but back here I got picked up by other people. Nobody wanted to hear the story, nobody would believe it.'

'What about your parents?'

'My mother's got a similar situation. Turns out my stepdad is a bad one too. We were trapped. Abused. Trapped. Can't get out of the cycle.'

'Do you want to be out?'

'More than anything,' said the woman. She was shaking. 'I don't know how. They'll come after you. You've seen what these people are like.'

'I could get you away, squirrel you out to somewhere, but I need your help with something. I need to understand something about Fredericks. You know he's dead.'

'I heard. But it isn't just Fredericks. It's his organisation. Some others involved—they're still there.'

'I take it you're still suffering the same fate?' asked Siobhan.

'Similar,' said Emma. 'I belong to him now. Sometimes, we go places. Sometimes, there are others to entertain. There's no way out of it. One of my friends, she killed herself. And they covered it up. She thought it would highlight it and bring them in to rescue the rest of us, but it didn't. You're the first person who's offered a way out. I don't know if you can do it, but I need you to do it.'

'Oh, I can do it,' said Siobhan. 'But you'll need to trust me. I can't get you out of here. It's not all set up yet. Where can you get to outside of your house? Somewhere public, somewhere I can grab you. Get you away.'

'Well, the only places I'm allowed to go are shopping for clothes, because they like me to look good, or to the gym and the swimming pool, because they like me to look good. Do you know what it's like to have a man like that? Just owns you. Doesn't want to know how you feel. Just wants to know how you look. Just wants to use you. Do you know what that's like?'

'Thankfully, not,' said Siobhan.

It made her think about Julian. She'd been struggling with him lately but was realising he had her best interests at heart, not simply what he wanted.

'When are you next at your sports centre? I need the address and I need a time. Women's changing rooms,' said Siobhan. 'We'll need to meet in there. It's the one place where we can meet with nobody around. Once we're in there, we can work our route out.'

'We normally go to the swimming pool first. I do several lengths, then I'll come in and shower. From there, I'll go to the gym. He waits for me in the gym, doesn't come into the pool. He watches me.'

'Well, we'll spot you in the pool, then. I'll have someone there to tell you if it's a go or not. If it is, we'll make an escape from the changing rooms. But he's got to go to the gym.'

'Sometimes he has others there. They like to meet at the gym and talk. He likes to show me off to them.'

'Doesn't matter,' said Siobhan. 'I'll get you out. Now, make sure you buy one of those tops.'

Siobhan stepped back out of the changing room, got to the doorway, and glanced around, looking for the man. He was standing about ten feet away, but thankfully had his back to her. She returned to Emma and pushed open on his curtain again.

'You'll have to go out first. He's there. Take him away, pay for that top you're carrying, I'll be able to nip out.'

'Sports centre, in town,' she said. 'Eight o'clock. I'll be in the pool from eight, we'll be in the gym from nine.'

'I'll see you there,' said Siobhan, ushering the woman out. Siobhan waited until she'd gone outside and then texted Kylie.

133

She replied that the woman was paying for her items along with the large man, and Siobhan disappeared back out into the store. She picked Kylie up in the far corner and the two of them disappeared back out into the city street.

'All good?' asked Kylie.

'She wants to run. I'm going to help her run tomorrow.'

'Run,' said Kylie. 'I thought you were looking for information.'

'Kylie, she's been effectively kidnapped. They look after her and that is her life. His plaything. She said that Fredericks was the one who looked after her first. After his death and getting away from England, she's been picked up by somebody of a similar vein. He might even be connected. We're going to get her out, Kylie. Can't leave a woman in that situation.'

'Of course,' said Kylie. 'What do you do with her afterwards?'

'We get ourselves a hidey hole. We put her in it and we operate from there. Get Julian in. He has ways and means and contacts. He used to work in the UK. My resources are not as plentiful as his.'

'At least, you can justify to him why you've gone this far then—why you need to go further,' said Kylie.

Siobhan looked away for a moment and then turned back to Kylie. 'Kylie, learn when it's good to say things to your boss. Julian and I are off limits. Case only.'

'Did I strike a nerve?' asked Kylie.

'Off limits,' said Siobhan.

Chapter 18

'And how's the last four hours been?' asked Julian.

'Long. Dull. Nothing's happened. He hasn't come out. He's still in that flat of his. I wish I was in that flat of his,' said Declan. 'I can see it now. Nice long sofa to lie in. Telly on. Probably watching the football. Maybe even watching some rock star. Gyrating. Moving their hips. Moving their—'

'If this is going places, can we just stop? I don't need details of what your sordid life would look like.'

'That's not fair. Man's just tired,' said Declan. 'Anyway, Mrs D wouldn't have me doing this.'

'Mrs D would have you doing this if she wanted,' said Julian. 'Go on, down to the car, get some sleep, as best you can.'

'I'm going to get some breakfast first. Do you want something?'

'Where are you getting it from?' asked Julian.

'Yellow Bear Muffin. All right?'

'We're in Belfast, Declan; get a soda, at least,' said Julian.

Half an hour later, Julian was fighting his way through two pieces of soda bread, bacon, sausage, egg, and anything else that could fit between them.

'Good these, aren't they?' said Declan.

Julian thought it was a heart attack on a plate, but it filled you up. Soda bread was a mystery to him. Siobhan once told him it was fighting bread because you could throw it at people, and it would probably knock them out, yet still be edible afterwards. It was the difference between an English breakfast and an Irish breakfast. A fantastic soda bread.

It was like potatoes in Ireland. You could serve three different types of potatoes at once and nobody batted an eyelid. He never got used to the place, though he had a deep fondness for it. Maybe he'd just been brought up in too reserved a fashion.

Once he finished the last of his soda, Julian chugged down some coffee, making sure that the bread made its way right down to his stomach. He looked up with his binoculars and saw Morrison on the move.

'Get the car.'

'Why?' asked Declan, only halfway through a soda.

'Because he's just grabbed his car keys. Get the car!'

Julian continued to watch Morrison until he got a phone call from Declan.

'He's about to come out. I think the car park's underneath. Get down there. I'll meet you at the front of the building.'

Julian ran down the concrete steps within the multi-storey car park and raced across the road to jump into the car, Declan having parked it up only moments before.

'He'll be coming out the back end. Next left,' said Julian.

They were fortunate enough to pick the man up, as his car disappeared out into the Belfast traffic. Declan followed under Julian's instruction, but as they cleared Belfast, Julian could see Declan looking down at the foot well.

'You've still got half your breakfast down there, haven't you?'

'Yes,' said Declan. 'You want something to eat?'

Julian shook his head. Declan had been good. He hadn't complained, and he was probably exhausted. But he was driving well.

Declan soon realised they were heading towards the Mourne mountains. The road headed out towards Saintfield and then cut back towards Newcastle. He wondered if he was going to head up to the mountains, but Morrison turned off into Newcastle, parking up along the seafront.

Newcastle was a strange place to Julian. You could see when the sun was out why people enjoyed it. There was the beach and lots of holidaymakers made their way out here. But a lot of the shops weren't really to Julian's cup of tea.

But there were the arcades, amusements, similar to Portrush in some ways, but without the extensive building full of rides. These were small arcades. Pennies dropped onto moving edges. Of course, these days the coinage had increased. There were slots as well. The occasional video game, too. They weren't what Siobhan had once described to Julian, but her memory was from back in the day when she was taken here as a child.

Morrison was sitting in his car, and Julian believed he was watching one particular arcade. The owner of that arcade was sitting behind a glass screen and handing out change. The man was a large individual. His gut was enormous and he didn't seem to move much away from the arcade itself.

It was round about lunchtime when he did hand over to someone else in the booth and almost waddled his way down the street. Julian wasn't for judging people, and he did not know what this man's life was like. But he saw Morrison get out and follow the man.

Julian jumped out of the car as well, telling Declan to come with him. They walked along the strand in front of the chip shops and coffee houses and watched as the large man entered one. He sat down looking out, and Julian told Declan to get some chips.

'I'm not hungry,' said Declan.

'Get some chips. We need some reason to be standing looking out to sea. We're two blokes. It's not a family outing.'

Julian watched as Morrison sat down in the cafe, too. Declan came back with the chips and the two of them sat on the seawall looking across.

'What's he doing?' asked Declan.

'Don't stare so,' said Julian. 'He's tailing him for something. I'm not sure what. He got that envelope the other night. He got instructions for something. I think this is it.'

'What sort of instructions?'

'I don't know,' said Julian; 'that's why we're watching.'

The large man continued to drink his coffee. Morrison was monitoring him. Julian watched as Morrison stood up, his hand in motion behind his back. Quickly, he walked past the large man's table. Julian saw his right hand swing out briefly, and then he was away again, off to use the facilities.

'What?' said Declan, looking at Julian's face.

'He's just dropped something into the coffee.'

'What?'

I said, "He's just dropped something into the coffee."

'What, like, you mean poison or something?'

'I don't know. I'm not that close.'

'Well, we need to warn him, then,' said Declan. 'That could be poison. That—'

'No, we don't,' said Julian.

'Yes, we bloody well do.'

'Don't get worked up,' said Julian.

'I'll damn well get worked up. We need to save that guy.'

'You know nothing about him. Let it be,' said Julian.

'We're not in the Service,' said Declan. He went to jump off the wall, but Julian put his hand out, holding him tight to it.

'Don't mention that word out loud. Don't move, don't flinch, don't get overexcited. Let it be.'

'You can't seriously tell me you're going to let someone die,' said Declan, his voice now hushed.

'I don't know what I'm going to do.'

'Well, I'm going over there,' said Declan. Julian left his chips on the wall and with both hands grabbed Declan's arm, putting it up his back. His right arm swung around Declan, and he marched him along the street as if they were simply out together having a laugh.

'What are you doing?' asked Declan furiously.

'I am keeping you and me safe,' said Julian. 'Nobody knows we're watching. Nobody has seen. For all you know, this could be a test. This could be—'

'He's poisoning someone.'

'Is he? Or is he just playing along?'

'But if he is—'

'If he is,' said Julian, 'the man will die.'

'Can't take that risk.'

'I'm prioritising here,' said Julian. 'Get in the car.'

They got into the car and Julian said he would drive. 'Put your seatbelt on. You step out of this car and I will knock you out,' said Julian. 'You go to save that guy. And I will fire you from ever working with Siobhan again.'

'But—'

'But nothing. Siobhan would agree with what I'm doing.'

'But we're not in that organisation,' said Declan, trying not to say the word.

'No, I'm not. I'm in Siobhan's team. And my job is to keep Siobhan's team safe, including me and Siobhan. We step in and act there, and we could walk into a trap. That man is not worth exposing ourselves.'

'You don't even know him.'

'Exactly. We don't,' said Julian.

He started the car up and drove to the end of the street, then turned round and drove back along the strand. As they passed the coffee house, he saw Morrison coming out. Julian tried to look in, but someone was standing in front of the window. He couldn't slow down, so he kept going.

'Where are we going?'

'I don't know. Back to watch them again. Possibly.' Julian pulled over as a text came in through from Siobhan.

'We're off to sort out some secret digs.'

'But Morrison's left. We could go back and save that guy.'

'No, it still stands,' said Julian. 'We go back, we could blow our cover.'

'But he could be walking around with poison in him.'

'Very much so. But I've told you, I'm protecting you.'

Declan went to react, but Julian started the engine again and drove off.

'We're going to find somewhere for everyone to hole up. Siobhan has got a woman that needs help and we need to get a secure house for her.'

'How do we do that?'

'I didn't work this place for this, for however long, without having a few up my sleeve.'

'But you can't leave that man.'

'I am and I have done. If we get tailed going to set up a secret house, we could end up endangering everyone. Siobhan believes we've got somebody worth protecting. We will protect her. Do you understand?'

'Okay,' said Declan. 'If that's the way you want it.'

'Don't get angry at me. That's the nature of this business. You don't like it, get out of it,' said Julian. 'Siobhan's taken us into some dark places. That's the type of investigation she wants to run. I'm not happy about it, but I'm here protecting you all. You don't want to be part of that, go back to your gardening, Declan. In fact, if I were you, I would go back to my gardening. The stuff we're involved in, it's not good. I'm trained for it, and I still want out of it.'

'But you came in with her. You went with Siobhan, helped her set up the agency Donaghadee.'

'Siobhan wants to be an investigator. She's not ready to stop yet. I was ready to stop when I left the Service. She was worth stopping for, but I can't stop her. I have to wait for her to stop.'

'You should tell Mrs D that.'

'Siobhan didn't get to where she is now without being able to work things out. She'll be able to read me. She'll get there when she makes her choice.'

'And if she doesn't want to give up,'

'Well, I'm with her to whenever,' said Julian. 'God knows it might cost me my life. But it shouldn't cost you yours. Or Kylie. The two of you should get out. You've a long life ahead of you.'

'So have you. You're only just into your fifties as well. How can you—'

'Because it's Siobhan, Declan. It's always been Siobhan for me. Don't you get that?'

The pair continued to drive until Declan was somewhere outside Belfast he didn't recognise. There was a small house hidden away from the road behind several trees. Julian pulled up in front of it, stepped out, disappeared off into the trees, and came back with a key and opened the front door.

'So, this is the secret pad, is it?'

'It is indeed. Nobody would find this,' he said. 'I've kept it off the books for years.'

'So what, we just wait here now?'

'No, we've got shopping to do. I don't keep somewhere like this with no food in it but it's only a couple of tins. We're going to have five people staying here. They need to be fed. So we'll do that. If we'd been tailed, I wouldn't have come here. We wouldn't have somewhere safe.'

They went inside, and Julian switched on the radio. It was the local station playing music and Declan seemed to sway to the music. Julian watched him as he made a cup of tea.

'Do you think you made the right call?' asked Declan.

'I made the only call,' said Julian. As he said so, the news came on the radio. There was an unexpected death in Newcastle, one of the amusement arcade owners.

'I made the only call,' said Julian. 'I hope one day you'll realise that, Declan. In case you have to make a similar one.'

Declan was looking out the window. Julian wasn't sure that it was a call that Declan could make.

Chapter 19

'And you're okay with the pack,' said Siobhan.

'Got a change of clothes in here. Got the wig,' said Kylie. 'Hopefully, we'll be able to get her out quickly.'

'I will be watching,' said Siobhan. 'But no risks. If you see him cause trouble, shout. Shout to everyone. I'll come in and sort it out.'

'Well, wish me luck then.'

'You don't need luck,' said Siobhan. 'You just need to use that head of yours. Okay?'

Kylie nodded and walked off into the sports centre. It was late at night now, but the sports centre was still busy. Siobhan entered as well, but heavily disguised, a brunette wig on, and glasses with large thick rims. She had tanned her face as well, not the normal pale skin people were used to seeing her in.

Kylie was making her way directly to the changing rooms for the gym, wearing a pair of leggings and a t-shirt. She wouldn't meet the woman in the swimming pool, but had left it to Siobhan to ID her.

Siobhan was sitting in the coffee area with a cup in front of her, watching the swimmers in the pool. It wasn't long before she spotted Emma with an entourage of large men around her.

Siobhan could see the man who had been so rude at the door that she jabbed her fingers into his throat.

Alongside him were another four men, all slightly different, one skinny, one even larger, but all looked like they could handle themselves. Siobhan wondered, *was this because of what had happened? Did the man suspect that Emma might run?*

They got away with it in the shopping centre when they met in the changing rooms. He couldn't be that worried, could he? But again, it wasn't every day that a woman came up to your house and roundly beat your backside to the ground. Siobhan realised that there were plenty of hard men about, but women who knew how to fight were less common, or at least used these skills less often. Not that the man knew how to fight—he clearly hadn't been trained that well.

Emma was wearing what Siobhan thought a man would buy her. The bikini certainly wasn't practical and Siobhan would be glad to get the woman out of this atmosphere.

She watched as Emma swam up and down under the watchful eye of the other men until she popped off to the changing rooms. Siobhan then watched as she left the swimming pool changing rooms and made her way over to the gym. The entourage followed, but she popped inside the women's changing area.

Siobhan drank her coffee, turned and walked down towards the changing rooms. She walked past them a few times and saw one of the accompanying men leave the male changing rooms and enter the gym.

Kylie would have to be quick, getting Emma changed. They would expect her inside any minute. There's only so long you could stretch, getting ready for. Only so long you could say that you were brushing your hair, sorting your ponytail out.

She would have to move and move soon.

Siobhan opened the door of the women's changing rooms, looked inside to see Kylie in the far corner, along with a red-headed Emma. Kylie put her thumb up. Siobhan nodded, left the room, and walked towards the door of the sports centre.

The car was parked out in the streets, not in the car park, because that gave a one line out to the road. Siobhan had parked it behind a lorry, which seemed to have been left there for the night. You'd have to be looking for Siobhan's car and get past the lorry before you saw it. The last thing she wanted was to be identified leaving the area.

Siobhan tapped her foot. Where were they? They needed to get on the move.

Siobhan watched the door of the changing rooms open. Kylie stepped out, looking left and right. She was followed down the corridor by Emma, the red wig looking slightly askew to Siobhan. Kylie turned towards the woman but as she did so, from out of the gym, stepped one of the men.

He took one look at Kylie, and then he looked at Emma. He said something out of earshot to Siobhan. Kylie flinched her shoulders casually, and said something to the man, who must have said something to her. Then his hand reached out and grabbed her.

The man shouted, calling for help, and Siobhan raced down the corridor. They were in a public place, so that might help. After all, you didn't just grab women. That kind of thing was frowned upon. But as Siobhan witnessed many times in her life, people didn't always react, either. They'd be much more likely to pull out a camera and film the event.

Kylie was putting up a good fight, swinging her open hand towards the man, slapping him, then driving her elbow in towards his stomach. However, he looked strong, and Siobhan wasn't sure she'd be able to break away.

Siobhan quickened her pace and saw beyond Kylie more men coming out. One of them took Emma by the hand, and tried to drag her back. Siobhan stepped past Kylie, and met another man coming towards her.

She didn't have time to get into a fight for several reasons. One, there were too many of them. Second, they were actually quite big. If she got held at all, she might not be able to protect herself or anyone else.

There was a punch coming towards Siobhan. She stepped to one side and jabbed the man in the throat. He stumbled backwards, and she brought her hand down hard on the arm of the man holding Emma. His grip loosened. She grabbed Emma and pulled her towards the corridor.

Beside her, Kylie was in the grip of the other man and Siobhan went to help, but found that Kylie had freed herself. Had it been a slap to the face? A push? Siobhan didn't care. She had to go and to go quickly.

She heard Kylie's footsteps behind her and the man chasing. Rather than go straight forward, Siobhan cut to the right, heading down another corridor, before descending stairs down into the depths. This was the access to sports courts. And she cut round and round, going this way and that, before she'd pass the boiler room.

'Where are we going?' asked Kylie.

'Out of one of these doors.'

Siobhan kept looking behind her, for the men were in pursuit and they weren't far away. She was trying to judge which door she could get out of and close before they would see her party. It wasn't easy since they were quite close behind.

Siobhan could hear Kylie panting, and she sucked in deep breaths as she ran. It wasn't easy. Although she was in decent shape, there were a lot of stairs and a lot of running. She passed one corner, but from the edge of her eye, saw a fire escape. She pulled Emma down the short corridor, pushed the fire escape door open, and spun round to see Kylie follow her out. Then, quickly but carefully, she shut the fire escape door.

'Where now?' said Kylie. Siobhan put a finger up to her mouth, showing Kylie should stay quiet.

'So,' said Siobhan, 'we wait a second.'

She listened to the door and heard footsteps, but they weren't coming closer. It looked like they'd gone past. She turned, grabbed Emma, and tore off across a football field. The field was in darkness, and Siobhan didn't slow her pace until she got to the far side. There, she pulled open a small gate in the wire fence and stepped outside onto the street.

'They'll be coming out in a minute, so quickly, but walk normally,' she said.

'Which is it?' asked Kylie.

Siobhan tutted, turned, and strode down the street. Two women followed her, but Siobhan's eyes were everywhere, looking for trouble. She cut down a side street and saw the large lorry that obscured the view of her car.

'You pair, stay about four steps behind me,' she said, wary in case anyone should jump out from behind the lorry. But no one was there, and she could click her keys, opening the car doors and tell everyone to get in. Once they were shut, Siobhan started the car, pulled out, and drove down the street.

'Are we all intact?' asked Siobhan.

'How did you get me out?' asked Emma. 'They were all

there.'

'it's what we do,' said Siobhan. 'it's what we do. Sit back; we'll take you somewhere, somewhere quiet.'

'You should probably get some rest,' said Kylie. 'I'm sure it's been tense all day today.'

Siobhan drove off into the Belfast night, but as she looked in the rear-view mirror, she saw their guest was not sleeping. Emma was eyes wide. Maybe she was frightened. Emma seemed to go into a slump, but she was thoughtful, too.

'You did well to get away from the man that grabbed you,' said Siobhan.

'I think he must have slipped,' said Kylie. 'He had a good hold of me and then all of a sudden he was going backwards.'

'Whatever you did, you did it right,' said Siobhan. She continued to drive right into the countryside.

'Where are we going?'

'Safehouse,' said Siobhan. 'Somewhere they can't get you.'

'Where is it?'

'You'll know it when you see it,' said Siobhan quietly, and settled down into the drive. The road was a single carriageway, and it ran up and down, over the drumlins that diminished in size as she came out of Belfast. As she went over the top of one of these, Siobhan took a hard left down a track, eventually reaching a farmhouse behind some trees, checking for Julian and Declan. The poor things hadn't arrived yet, whatever they were up to.

Siobhan parked the car up behind some trees, so it couldn't be seen from the road. Stepping out, feet crunched in the gravel, she made her way to the front door. She reached down under a flowerpot, pulled out a key, and told everyone else to wait outside while she went in. She's did a quick sweep of the house. As expected, there was no one, and she then put on some lights before closing the curtains.

'Make something, Kylie. Quite hungry after that,' said Siobhan. 'Make our guest something too. A cup of lapsang souchong for me, please.'

Siobhan made her way over to the sofa, sat down on it and pondered. Everything had gone smoothly, very well. She'd expected a bit more resistance, but maybe they were simple thugs; maybe they weren't operators. Siobhan wondered, but she had to say she was looking forward to Julian getting there. She was almost happy operating on her own, but you didn't get any extra.

How badly in were they this time? Who were these people? Hopefully, in the coming days, they would know.

Chapter 20

Siobhan felt her eyes beginning to close when her mobile phone vibrated in her pocket. She took it out to see that it was Declan calling, and she answered it.

'Hello, Mrs D. We'll be there shortly.'

'Everything okay, Declan?' asked Siobhan, for his voice sounded down.

'It's been a bit of a rough one,' he said, 'but we're fine. Not to do with us, just something I saw.'

'Okay,' said Siobhan. 'Well, get to the safe house; you can have a good rest.'

Siobhan closed the call, and Kylie stepped into the room. 'Was that Declan.'

'Yes. He sounded a wee bit down.'

'Is he okay?' asked Kylie.

'Nothing that seeing you won't put right.'

Kylie gave her a look but then sat down on the sofa beside Siobhan. Opposite, Emma was sitting and yawning.

'You don't mind if I go up and have a lie down?' said Emma. 'I'm just exhausted. That was all quite—how would you put it?'

'Yes, it was, wasn't it?' said Siobhan. 'You going up?'

'I'll take the bedroom at the back.'

She watched the woman get up, and she took her bag with her. It was overly clean. It had her swimming stuff in it, and she'd been carrying it when they'd escaped.

'What's up with Declan then?' asked Kylie, as Emma left the room.

'He said he had a rough day. He said he's fine. They're fine. Just something he saw.'

'He likes to think he's a lot stronger than he is,' said Kylie. 'He puts on a brave face at times but underneath it churns him up.'

'Not the only one that happens with,' said Siobhan.

'It's not what happens with Julian, is it? Julian's so calm.'

'Julian has a perfect exterior,' said Siobhan. 'But inside, he's the same as the rest of us. Vulnerable. Get under the shell. He's just the same as you and me.'

'Well, he's a lot faster than me. Thinks a lot quicker. And can take people out,' said Kylie. 'Bit of a difference.'

Siobhan smiled. Then looked over at the empty seat.

'What's the matter?' asked Kylie.

'Would you have grabbed your bag on the way out?'

'Maybe. If you're going to run, maybe it's got a few keepsakes in it. Things you don't want to leave behind. Maybe set you wrong. Anyway, Declan will be here soon with Julian. I had a chat with Julian about what happened to us. You said that guy that was holding you just fell back. Did you push him at all?'

'I was pushing. I'm not sure I was strong enough to do what happened.'

She stood up, wandered over to the window, and pulled back the curtain. A car was pulling into the drive, and she recognised it. Siobhan watched it pull up and two figures got out. Everyone smiled.

She was ready to see Julian again, despite the differences of opinion they were having at the moment. She didn't meet him at the door, but instead walked into the lounge, heard a key in the lock, and then Declan's smiling face came into the room. Kylie was up off the seat, running over to him and throwing her arms around him. Julian was more subtle as he entered, but he made his way over towards Siobhan, who stood up and hugged him.

'Declan said you had a bit of a rough time today.'

She whispered this in Julian's ear, and he whispered back, 'Had to let somebody die. Could have blown the cover.'

Siobhan nodded and then looked over at Declan. He was happy in the arms of Kylie.

'Where's our girl?' asked Julian.

'She's upstairs—Emma. I think we're going to need to have a talk. I've got a few doubts,' said Siobhan.

'A few doubts? In what way?'

'Well,' said Siobhan. 'We got her out. There were a lot of guys. I fought some of them off. Had to be quick about it. But Kylie got away from one of them. He was far too strong for her. She's not sure how she did it. She's not sure how he—'

'You're not over-reading this, are you?' asked Julian.

'It's not just that,' said Siobhan. 'We also have Emma leaving with her bag'

'Well, that's not unreasonable. She might have had something in it. She's leaving a life, maybe there was something she needed to take into the next life with her. It's not unreasonable.'

'No, but the holes are lining up, aren't they?'

At that point, Emma entered the room. She smiled as she

152

walked over to the window.

'Don't open the curtains,' said Siobhan. 'You need to keep away from all the windows. You, especially. You need to—'

Siobhan saw some headlights and some cars coming down the drive.

'Julian!'

Julian ran to the front door, closely followed by Siobhan.

'Four or five cars. We'll not get our cars out past them. We need to go out the back.'

'Declan, grab Emma. Let's go,' said Siobhan. She went to run as she heard people getting out onto the stone driveway, coming towards the house. Declan was already out towards the rear door. Siobhan stopped, looking at Declan. He was pulling at Emma, but Emma wasn't moving. Kylie was screaming at Declan, telling him to come on.

'Declan, just go, leave her,' said Siobhan, realising what was up. But Emma was now holding Declan. The door behind Siobhan was suddenly hit hard from the outside and splintered.

Siobhan looked, but Julian was already out the door. Other people were now piling in. Siobhan turned to Declan, shouting at him. Siobhan ran, but met a man in front of her. He went left as she went right. She kicked him hard towards the knees, then hit him with a few punches. But her progress was slowed down.

She was grabbed from behind as more people piled into the house. Siobhan glanced to her left. She saw Declan being jumped, Kylie being thrown across the room. Siobhan knew she had to escape.

Kylie and Declan were grabbed, and her heart sank, wondering what it would mean for them. Who were these people? She knew Emma had brought them and she was cursing herself for not reacting to her suspicions earlier, but she didn't have time to think now.

She drove an elbow into the stomach of another man and then, as someone behind her grabbed her, she bit into his hand. There were too many of them. This was going to be a dirty fight.

She grabbed the man in front by the hair, driving his head into the wall. She felt something hit her in the back of the leg. Hit again in the back, she fell down to the ground as someone kicked her in the face. The world seemed to spin, but she was trying to get herself back up.

Someone grabbed her arm, driving it up her back, causing her to shout out. Where was Julian? She needed Julian now. He needed to come to her rescue.

A second set of hands grabbed her other arm and soon Siobhan was being lifted, taken back through to the living room. Siobhan looked up and the man who she had driven her fingers into at Emma's house, was standing before her.

He delivered a blow with the back of his hand that nearly took Siobhan's head off. She was shaking now. What was going to happen? Would Julian get back to save them?

She was driven to her knees. Again she looked up at the man and he slapped her again. Her head slumped forward, but it was held up and allowed the man to slap her one more time. He then moved over to Kylie. He didn't slap her, but placed his hand under her chin and squeezed her cheeks.

'She's got the looks. They could take her away,' said the assailant, at which point Declan spat on him. The man delivered a blow with the back of his hand to Declan that nearly knocked him out. He slumped forward. Siobhan told him to stop it.

'Not so big now, are you, missus?' said the man. 'Not clever. Emma's always been under my control. She's my girl, do you hear that? Do you? Hope you're not one of these have-a-go heroes.'

'Where's the other guy?' shouted someone.

'What do you mean?'

'Two of them. Two guys came into the house,' said Emma. 'What's the other one's name? Julian, she called him.'

Siobhan's head was lifted by her hair, and the man put his face close to hers. 'Where is Julian?'

Siobhan looked at him. She then looked at Emma and she laughed.

'What are you laughing about?'

'You let him go. He's got out. You hit me, he will rain a fire on you like you have never felt.'

'You're his, are you? Oh well. I look forward to this.'

The blood trickled out from the side of her mouth, but she continued to laugh. 'You secured only a couple of us,' said Siobhan. 'You let go of the most dangerous one.'

'He's not very chivalrous, is he? Not very kind, or good at protecting you guys. Didn't look after his woman.' Another slap came across Siobhan's face.

'He'll come for you. He'll come for all of you now. Watch out!' said Siobhan.

Siobhan could hear footsteps crunching on the gravel outside, doors opening. And almost a reverent hush formed in the room. She twisted her head, ringing as it was for the blows delivered to it.

A man walked in. A man in a tailored suit, clearly with money. And she thought she recognised Randolph Frederick.

Chapter 21

Siobhan wondered who the man was. He looked like Randolph Frederick, but Randolph Frederick was dead. There'd been a police investigation. He looked smart though, but he wasn't for saying a lot. Siobhan and her team were grabbed, tied to chairs, and placed in front of Emma. She was smirking now.

'I was waiting for a chance to show them I could be trusted, and you gave it to me, so frankly I should say thank you to you. We had to move quick though. I think you were beginning to suspect.'

'Who is she exactly?'

'I told you who I was,' said Siobhan. 'My name is Siobhan Duffy of Gold Coast Investigations.'

'Maybe I should introduce myself,' said the man in the smart suit who had come in. 'Randolph was my brother. My name is Xavier, and I want to know why you're looking into the practices of the fund.'

'I'm looking into the death of a client's brother. Alex Samuels.'

The man shook his shoulders. Then he looked at Emma. She shook her head as well. He looked across at one of the men. But no one was offering anything up.

'Alex Samuels. Never heard of him.'

'Lived in Belfast. Posh flat. Had a picture of your brother. Well, more a video, in an uncompromising position,' said Siobhan. 'I thought you might have been there.'

'It seems you are barking up the wrong tree,' said Xavier. 'I don't know why this man had a video of my brother, but maybe we can find out.'

'He died in Tollymore Forest Park, in the Hermitage,' said Siobhan.

Suddenly, the man's interest was piqued. 'Tollymore?' he said. 'The Hermitage?' Emma turned to him. She seemed to whisper something.

'You're right, Emma,' said Xavier. 'The Fox.'

'Who's the Fox?' asked Declan. He was slapped across the face.

'I'm talking to your boss,' said Xavier. 'Do be quiet. Right, you're investigating the Fox. Why?'

'Who's the Fox?' asked Siobhan.

'You don't know, do you? You tell me you've come this far, and you don't know who the Fox is? He's a hired killer, works in secret. He dispatched my brother.'

'Alex Samuels dispatched your brother?' queried Siobhan. 'Are you sure it was him?'

'It was one of them. I'm sure that one of a group of them did it. It may have been the Golden Queen; it may have been him, but the Fox is now dead. I just need to work out who did it. Find the rest of the group.'

'Wow,' said Siobhan. 'I didn't know any of that. So, I'm looking into the death of a hitman.'

Xavier laughed. 'You really are behind the curve, Miss Duffy, aren't you? Way behind the curve.'

'Mrs Duffy!' said Siobhan. 'Maybe I am, but we'll catch up.'

'No, you won't,' he said. 'You see, you've been poking your nose into our business. We don't like people examining what we do.'

'Is that because you take some rather lovely young women and use them for your own purposes? It's clever though, you actually do some good as well. I like that one,' said Siobhan.

Siobhan's wrists were firmly tied behind her and she was trying to work out how to get out. She didn't have a razor blade; she didn't have anything with which to untie her hands. They'd bound them well. They'd also now tied her feet to the chair. She had no other options. It wasn't like she could fight her way out like this. There were plenty of people. As Xavier turned and went to the window, pushing back the curtains, he looked out.

'Your friend didn't take the cars. I guess we blocked them off. He won't get anywhere. We'll get him.'

Siobhan let go a smile. 'Really? Do you know who he is?'

'Enlighten me.'

'Julian was one of the finest,' she said. 'He worked for the Service. I'm sure you'll have heard of them.'

'The Service. The Service tried to investigate us. We were able to keep them out of the way. Uninterested. That's what a lot of it's about. Keeping the profile, making sure you're not anybody to them. Meanwhile, you carry on with all your activities. I'd love to share it all with you, explain how we do it. Not because I want you to learn, because I like to brag. Trouble is, it might be safest to dispose of you and your friends. What are you? Some investigators getting themselves on the wrong side. People won't bat an eyelid if you end up in trouble.'

'Julian will come for us.'

Xavier looked out the window again. 'I've got all my men out looking for him. He won't get far. Nowhere to go. So, he'll probably do what a lot of them do, hang about hoping they can rescue you, instead of going far away, making sure they get clear. It's a mistake. Sometimes you have to cut your losses.'

'Sometimes your losses are too great,' said Siobhan. 'Have you ever had somebody looking for vengeance come after you?'

'Of course,' said Xavier. 'That's why I hire bodyguards. That's why I hire the best, to kill them first. Think on your last words, Mrs Duffy, because as soon as we find your colleague, I fear I'll have to despatch you. I'll keep you alive until then. Always good to bargain with; always good if we need to bring him in.'

'You won't have to bring him in,' said Siobhan. 'He'll find you. He'll kill you before you even know it.'

Xavier walked up and slapped Siobhan. 'You keep out of my business. I have a feeling about you,' he said. 'You wouldn't keep out of anything, would you? Will see it to the end. You're that sort of person. Ex-service as well, I expect. It's the only way he would have told you. Only way you would have known.' He laughed. 'Well, anyway, at least you'll be trained to die. It's time to wait for him.'

The man suddenly reached for his phone and looked at the screen.

'I'm afraid to tell you, Mrs Duffy, that your partner is dead. We found him and dispatched him. I'm sorry for your loss.'

Siobhan's heart sank for a moment. She wouldn't believe it. She just simply wouldn't believe it. Julian? Not like that.

159

'I won't let you suffer for long. Obviously it's an enormous shock to lose your colleague. Would you like me to dispose of you first? One, two, or three. Maybe I could knock them out so they wouldn't see you die. I'm a kind man in that regard.

'You just got caught in something that was too big for you. Something you couldn't handle. You really should look for some backup.'

He stepped to the side of Siobhan and pulled a gun from within his coat, and pointed it at Siobhan's head.

'Well, I guess this is farewell. If you come back in the next life, don't take an interest in other people. It can be the death of you.'

Siobhan looked to her right, where Xavier was standing. 'Stop,' she said.

'Why would I stop?' said Xavier.

'Look at your chest.' The man looked down. There was a red dot right where his heart was.

'Put the gun down. He won't wait long. He's given you a chance and he'll rip through everyone.'

Xavier started to shake.

'It's a trick,' said Emma.

'It's no trick, I'm telling you,' said Siobhan.

'It's definitely a trick,' said Emma. 'I'll stand in front of you. I'll—'

'Well played, Mrs Duffy. Well played. I think there's more to you than meets the eye,' said Xavier.

'Get these ropes untied now, or I'll give him the signal to shoot.'

'You tell him to shoot, you'll be dead,' said Emma.

'No,' said Siobhan. 'He'll be able to react. He can take out a room full of people before they can move. I don't think he's that far away.'

Siobhan watched as one of the large men was ordered by Xavier to untie her bonds. She stood up, took the gun from Xavier's hand and threw it into the corner of the room. Turning back, she watched as Kylie and Declan were also untied. She walked up to the man she had first met at Emma's house and delivered a back-of-the-hand blow across his face. She then turned and slapped Emma hard. Then Siobhan stood before Xavier.

'You come after any of my people, I see you harm any of them, and I will come for you. I'm ex-Service too. We'll both come for you. There'll be no leash on us. It'll be straight revenge. And shame on you for hitting a woman.'

She slapped him hard across the face. The red dot was still on the chest. She turned.

'Kylie, Declan, go!'

She led them outside, where a number of bodies lay on the ground. Cars had been cleared from their own vehicles' path by someone and Siobhan got Declan to drive Kylie whilst she drove the other car out onto the road. Siobhan drove a good two hundred metres away before signalling to Declan to park up with her. Kylie got out of the car and ran up towards Siobhan. Siobhan rolled down the window.

'What's up? Something wrong with the car?' asked Kylie.

'Nope. Julian will get in very shortly. And then we have to go off to another safe house. Somewhere safer than that.'

Siobhan looked at Kylie. She was shaking. Her eyes were watering.

'Get in the car with Declan. We'll be on the move in a minute. There'll be time for that later.'

Siobhan waited, and it was only thirty seconds later that the car door opened and Julian jumped in. She drove off, Kylie and Declan following her in the car behind.

'Did you miss me?' Julian said.

'He said we were getting in with big people. Perhaps someone should have told me,' said Siobhan.

'I did.'

'Well, I think you could be right.'

Chapter 22

The following morning, Siobhan awoke in a small farmhouse. Julian had called in a favour and at three in the morning, they'd all settled down for the night. Declan and Kylie were shaking. Julian was more perturbed. He'd been restless through the night, Siobhan catching him several times, standing up at the window of the small farmhouse they were in. She'd got out of the bed every time and rubbed his shoulders.

He told her to go back to bed. Not nastily, just said he needed to think. She hadn't bothered returning, at least not until she'd held him for a bit. She wondered what he must make of all this. Finally, they were getting a time together. But what a time, running here and there and everywhere. They'd retired from the service, and yet they seemed to be in as much trouble now as they ever were. Gold Coast Investigations was barely off the ground, and it had nearly lost all of its team.

The following morning, after a shower, Siobhan came downstairs to see Declan and Kylie still looking somewhat shaken. However, Julian was on his laptop.

'We're going to find out about the Fox,' he said. 'You need to give me half a day. I suspect you might have to look after these two. They're not right. Besides, you've all got some wounds to tend to.'

This was true. Siobhan had looked in the mirror, and she was heavily bruised on one side of her face. Declan too. Kylie had probably got away the lightest of the three of them, but her wrists were sore. They had tied the bonds tight—extremely tight. Not that it bothered Siobhan. But for someone as delicate as Kylie, it hurt.

The rest of the morning was spent with the radio on and making sure that Kylie and Declan took a bath. This was to make sure they were relaxed before Siobhan asked them to talk about the previous night. There wasn't much to say. About halfway through the conversation, Kylie suddenly blurted out she thought Siobhan was going to be dead. Tears started to flow, and Siobhan had to hold her before Declan came in.

'What about you, Declan?' asked Siobhan. 'Did you think I was going to die?'

Over Kylie's sniffs, Declan surprised her. 'Mrs D, you're never going to die. You guys know what you're doing.'

Did he really not get how close they'd come to messing it all up the previous night? Did he really think she was that good?

Just after lunch, Julian arrived back with some freshly made sandwiches and a box of lapsang souchong.

'You're a godsend. You know that,' Siobhan said to Julian, giving him a kiss.

'We need to sit down and have a talk about this.'

'Why, what's up?'

'All of us,' said Julian.

The four of them sat around a small wooden table in the kitchen and ate the sandwiches. Kylie made the tea, giving Siobhan her cup of lapsang souchong which she drank heartily.

'I've been speaking to some contacts about the Fox and they've got rumours of his participation in several murders, but I've got a problem.'

'What?' asked Siobhan.

'The Fox has killed since Alex died.'

'Really?'

'How does that work, then?' said Declan. 'That's definitely Alex, isn't it? We know Alex died.'

'That's what he's identified as. Yes. After all, Kieran did ID him for the police as well,' said Julian.

'So, the Fox is still at large,' said Siobhan. 'Alex wasn't the Fox then. Alex was somebody like the Fox, but not quite.'

'That doesn't make sense,' said Julian, 'does it?' Siobhan shook her head.

'Why?' said Declan.

'You're talking about a top-end hitman. Top-end killer,' said Julian. 'They protect their names.'

'Well, was Alex using it then, and that's why they killed him?' asked Declan.

'Not much of an example though, is it? It's taken us how long to work out who he is? And besides, the Fox would have had a team. Hitmen are never one person, there's always somebody that feeds into them. There's always somebody that stands between them and the interested party. Maybe Alex was the middleman?'

'Very hard to prove, now,' said Siobhan. 'You'd have to have found somebody prepared to say they ordered a hit and how. They will not do that. They'd have to find the Fox themselves. They will not admit to anything. Or even being the Fox. It's getting kind of awkward now, isn't it?'

'It's getting very awkward,' said Julian. 'Every time we get anywhere close, things are clamping down.'

'What do you think we should do, then?' asked Siobhan.

'I think we walk,' said Julian. 'I think we walk.'

'But we're stuck here, aren't we? I mean, we're hiding out.'

'Hiding out from who?' asked Julian.

'From Randolph's brother. Hiding out from Xavier, aren't we?' mused Siobhan.

'Yes, Xavier's worried because we're going after him. We've been investigating him. We could call a truce on that and walk away. Let's face it, we have got nothing. He must know that. He let us in, trapped us because we were investigating. All we've got is rumour and conjecture. We have got nothing definite.'

'That guy tried to kill us. He said it was better just to dispose of us,' said Kylie.

'He did. But he didn't know who we were then. I can work a truce,' said Julian. 'I can get us to walk away.'

'What about Kieran though?' said Siobhan. 'He hired us.'

'Well,' said Julian, 'think about it. If you tell Kieran about his brother, about his brother's death and what he was, if he tries to get involved, it'll mean his own death. These people will not take kindly to another nose being put in, will they? They're not going to say, "Oh look, come in; we'll have tea and biscuits and have a chat about it. Oh, your brother, yes, this is what he did." Maybe the brother, Alex, was cut out for a reason. They could end up closing Kieran down as well.'

'That's the crux of it though, isn't it?' said Siobhan. 'We still don't know why he died.'

'We may never know why he died. Something I can live with,' said Julian.

'I agree,' said Declan. 'I could live with that.' Kylie nodded.

'Well, I don't know about me,' said Siobhan. 'I took on the case. Was hired to solve it. I thought the least I could do was tell him why his brother is dead.'

'Siobhan, can I have a moment with you alone?' said Julian.

'Come on, Declan,' said Kylie. She took his hand and left the room with him. Julian stood up from behind the table.

'You get this?' he said. 'We're walking in to hired killers.'

'You and I have dealt with them before,' said Siobhan.

'They haven't. And when I've dealt with them, we've dealt with them with the force of the Service behind us. This is not something to do,' said Julian. 'I am retired, Siobhan. I am completely retired. I am out of the Service. You? You traded the Service for Gold Coast Investigations. You never left. You are still trying to either right wrongs or solve issues with people. At the heart of it, you just want to be involved. You can't lay it down!'

'That's not true.'

'Really? You're about to walk into this,' said Julian. 'You're about to walk into this. You're about to lead a man possibly to his own death by trying to show him where his brother died. This is not a world he needs to be in. It's not a world I want to be in. We're not as sharp as we used to be.'

'You're sharp. You might not be as physically fit, but you're sharp. Always were and still are.'

'That won't work,' said Julian. 'I'm not being sucked into this. Look,' he said. 'I'll follow you. I left the Service for you and I will follow you. Don't take those kids with you. Don't take them with you!'

Siobhan stood up, and wrapped her arms around Julian. 'Do you want me to quit this?'

'That's what I've been saying.'

167

'Well,' she said. 'You may be right. But I keep the agency. I keep the—'

'Okay,' said Julian. 'Keep the agency, but you don't take on something like this. Go back to simple things, basics. Train those two up to be decent investigators. Not running around into this sort of nonsense. Normal, run-of-the-mill stuff. Make that your goal. Make it about them, not about you. Maybe you'll be happy that way.'

'This is what you want?' said Siobhan.

'It's why I left. I didn't leave to come back and do the same thing over and over again. People are wondering what I'm doing. I'm using my contacts all the time. They think there's been a big lie that I've left the Service. It's a game that I'm still playing. Trouble is, it feels like a game until something goes wrong. I had to stop Declan from saving a man from dying. From using every good judgement he had. I don't want to turn that kid into me.'

Siobhan hugged him tightly. 'We will stop,' she said. 'We'll stop. You sort it with the Fredericks. Make them know we're no threat, and we'll walk away.'

'Good,' said Julian and kissed her on the head.

The radio was still on in the background when a newsflash came on.

'The Head of the Frederick's family has been found dead after a fire. Xavier Fredericks was burned to death in a—'

The words came out of the radio quickly and it took Siobhan's brain a moment to catch up.

'Did that just say what I thought it said?'

'It did,' said Julian.

'It's going to make it a lot easier, isn't it?'

'You might just have somebody looking after you up there,'

said Julian. Siobhan hugged him tightly. 'I'll tell the other two. We'll bring them in here and I'll tell them. It's going to wreck Declan's image of me, though,' said Siobhan.

'Well, you've just enhanced the image I have of you,' said Julian, 'and that wasn't too shabby to begin with.'

'You're right,' she said to Julian. 'I miss it. I always want to charge after it, solve it, work it out, but the cost is too much. It always was. It always will be.'

'Good,' said Julian. 'Time now to make peace and get back to the office.'

Chapter 23

Siobhan re-entered the offices of Gold Coast Investigations, in a sad mood. She never liked to be beaten, never liked for anything to have got away from her. But as she stepped across the threshold of the offices, she knew she was doing it for good reason.

Behind her, Julian touched her shoulder, following her into the office.

'Good to be back, Mrs D,' said Declan. 'I'll go make sure the supplies are done.'

'Get the kettle on, Kylie, please,' said Siobhan, and walked straight upstairs towards her office.

'Is she okay?' asked Kylie.

'She will be,' said Julian. 'She will be. Doesn't enjoy being beaten. Doesn't like having to withdraw from something.'

Siobhan stood in her office and looked around at what were still freshly painted walls. She needed a picture for the far side. She'd been right about the flowers, though. They were dead. She popped them into the bin and resolved to get another bunch later on that day. She slipped into her chair behind her desk with a large computer in front of her.

What to do? She'd need to wait for the next case now. She'd

need to get something else to come through the door. Were there any emails? She looked up. *Nothing of note*, she thought. Oh, somebody's cat's gone missing. She huffed a bit. Then she heard a rap at the door.

'I've got this for you,' said Kylie. She placed a cup of lapsang souchong in front of Siobhan. 'Not a bad view out today,' Kylie said, stepping behind Siobhan and looking out the window. 'There are a couple of boats in the harbour. The wind's not too strong either. A bit of sun breaking out. There's also—'

'You don't have to sit here and try to lift my mood, okay? I'll come round.'

'Okay,' said Kylie. She turned to walk to the door and Siobhan spoke after her.

'Kylie, look, I'm appreciative but it won't work and I have to come round in my time. It's the way I am. Thank you for trying.'

'Julian said it wouldn't work.'

'Well, he's known me a lot longer.'

'I'm kind of glad to be out of that, though. It was exciting, but it was only exciting to that point where we were tied up.'

'I didn't like the bit where he put the gun to my head,' said Siobhan. 'I've got to admit, I wasn't buzzing at that point.'

The trouble was, and Siobhan knew it, she had been buzzing at that point. She was absolutely buzzing, her mind racing to work out how to get out of the situation. She was alive when faced with these situations. Now, here back in the office, there was no buzz. What should she do?

Wait for somebody to come in and tell her all about their spouse? Her wavering husband, who was disappearing at night. She wasn't sure where he was going. Siobhan would stand on stepladders, taking photographs into bedrooms. Or would she have to work out who was sending the threatening letters? It's all riff-raff, all nonsense, all tripe. *Come on, Siobhan,* she thought to herself. *Catch yourself on.*

She stood up and walked over to her door, looking into the office across from hers. Julian was sitting back with his feet up on the desk. He was whistling a small tune. She decided not to disturb him and instead turned back to her desk to start planning the day. *Flowers,* she thought. *I could go get the flowers.*

'We're going through the post,' said Kylie from downstairs.

'And?' shouted Siobhan.

'Well, got bills. The painter and decorator.'

'That's fine,' said Siobhan. 'Just pay them.'

I've also got to talk to Kieran, she thought. *I'll need to phrase that delicately. How do I explain it away, in a way that he won't go after anyone?*

She stood up, hearing the door downstairs, wondering who had come in. When she got to the landing, she glanced down the stairs, and saw it was just a postie. He dropped off a box. Quite small, more like a parcel.

'This one's for you,' said Kylie, 'like everything that comes into this place, all for you.'

'Nothing for me?' said Julian.

'Well, there's something here about stairlifts. Did you order that?' asked Kylie.

Julian came to the stairs and looked down. 'That's not funny.' He popped down though, picked up the parcel and returned up the stairs to give it to Siobhan.

'I can run up and down the stairs myself,' she said.

'Just keeping busy,' said Julian. He turned and went into his office.

'You're not wanting to know what this is?'

'Of course not,' said Julian. 'It's got your name on it. It's for you. Not for me. I mean, it could be anything. Maybe sexy underwear you've ordered for my birthday.'

'Sexy underwear for you or for me?' said Siobhan.

'Matching set,' said Julian, laughing, and walked off back to his office.

Siobhan put the parcel down on the desk and took another sip of lapsang souchong. It was always comforting. She never understood why other people didn't like it. Just because it was smoky. It was a reassuring brew, something that you always came back to.

Siobhan took a pair of scissors and cut the side of her parcel. Reaching in, she found an envelope and took it out. Opening the envelope, she found a letter inside. Printed.

'You should have stayed away,' it said. 'Your time is coming. Your time is almost here.'

Siobhan instantly grabbed the small package and threw it inside a bin. She then turned the bin up and pushed it against the wall. There was a minor explosion, not enough to force the bin out of her hands, but enough for it to cause her to jump. She moved the bin back off the wall. It was full of glitter. But inside was also a small tube.

Julian was across in a flash. 'What on earth was that?' he asked.

'There was a letter in the package, said my time had come. "You should have stayed away." I put it up against the wall and it went off. I don't know what's the deal with it, but—'

'Is there anything else inside?' asked Julian.

'Glitter, as far as I can see.'

'A glitter bomb.'

'Somebody making a point. Somebody's showing they can

173

get to us.'

'Anything else in there, though? It's a statement, but it's not much of a statement.'

'I can see a tube,' she said.

'Careful now. Let's have a look,' said Julian.' He took the tube out and stared at it. Slowly, he undid the cork. A piece of paper was inside and Julian tapped it out. Siobhan opened it and Julian took a photograph of it.

'What's it say?' he asked.

'It says that we've been offered to the group.'

'What group?'

'It says we've been offered to the group, and the Fox is after the chickens.'

Julian stepped back for a moment. 'Wow. We are going to have to finish this the old-fashioned way,' he said.

Siobhan reeled. She stepped over to the window and looked out, scanning the street. There was no one there. There was no reason that somebody had to deliver the package. It could have been sent through the mail. The postie could have been genuine. After all, it was simply a glitter bomb. If it had been intercepted, people would have said it's just a harmless prank.

'I wanted out,' said Siobhan.

'No, you didn't. You came out,' said Julian. 'Entirely different.'

'Somebody's not letting me come out. Sorry, dear, but I think we're in this one to the end.'

'But who? And why the Fox?' asked Julian.

'He's talking about being hired,' said Siobhan. 'The Fox is after the chickens. We've been offered to the group. Offered? Paid for? What the hell does that mean, Julian?'

'I'll tell you what it means. It means we're going to have to

174

look after those two downstairs. This isn't good. This is not good at all. On the bright side,' said Julian, 'at least, I haven't unpacked.'

Chapter 24

'Right, everyone, that's it. Pack up.'

'What?' said Declan. 'We've only just arrived. You haven't even replaced your flowers, Mrs D.'

'And I won't be replacing them, Declan. We're shutting up again.'

'Why?'

Siobhan relayed the details of what happened upstairs.

'We got a warning,' said Julian, 'and we need to heed it, and we need to get out of here quick.'

'Declan, grab your stuff with Kylie from the house. We'll follow you back there, and then we head off somewhere.'

'Where?' asked Declan.

'Somewhere special,' said Julian. 'This has got beyond dangerous.'

'Is this going to work out all right, Mrs D?' asked Declan.

'Do you want me to lie to you?'

'That would be good.'

'It's all going to be wonderful, Declan.'

Kylie walked up to Siobhan, staring at her. 'This isn't good, is it? This really isn't good.'

'No, it's not good at all,' said Siobhan. 'But we'll beat it. We will beat it.'

Julian followed them all back in his car until they came to the house by the sea. Siobhan disappeared into her bedroom, packed a few things, and they then picked up Kylie and Declan from the lodge, having packed their belongings. Nobody had much with them, and Siobhan hoped it wouldn't be a long stay, but Julian had been right. It was the right call to make.

'Okay,' said Julian. 'This place I'm going to, you never tell anyone about it, ever. This is the last stop. This is the one that was set up for me in case I ever got into real trouble. There are a lot of things about it that are beyond normal.'

Julian approached a house deep in the countryside. The path down to it swung amongst different trees. Declan sat back, almost enjoying himself with the intrigue.

'I get this is out in the country,' said Kylie, 'but how is this any better than anywhere else?'

'Because if you come to this house, I have it well defended.' Julian parked the car and got out. He watched as Declan made his way closer to the house. He stepped off the path to move round to the right. Julian grabbed him. 'Nope, not that way.'

'Why not?'

'Because it will blow. Okay.'

Julian walked up to the door, took out a key, but before he put it in, he pressed a button at the side. A flap went up and Julian had his retina checked. Once he'd opened the door, he stepped inside and asked each of them to put their retina up to the scanner.

'You can't get in without the key and an eyeball,' he said. 'Don't forget that. I can get you all a key, not a problem.'

'Is this all really necessary?' asked Declan.

'Just go inside for the minute,' said Julian. 'We'll talk about it inside.'

It was a rather spacious kitchen, and Julian invited everyone in. He made drinks for everyone.

'You're asking if this is essential. No.'

The interior of this house of Julian's was well laid out. The furnishings weren't lavish; they were practical, but they were also comfortable. There was a TV which Declan put on, but Julian switched it back off.

'Everyone in the kitchen. Sit down, we're going to talk.'

'You heard the man,' said Siobhan. 'In we go.'

The four of them then sat around the kitchen table, and together they discussed what was happening.

'We've got a note,' said Julian. 'A note delivered. A small explosive. That was a warning. That was just to get us bothered.'

'Are we bothered? Is that what we call it?' asked Declan.

'We are resolved,' said Julian.

'We are pissed off,' said Siobhan. 'I was this close to walking away, this close to being out of it, and had settled myself into agreeing with that decision. And then this happens. You don't threaten me. I will sort them.'

'We're in real trouble,' said Julian. He looked at Kylie and Declan. 'We are in real trouble. I need to protect you two, especially. It looks like we have a hitman after us. On that basis, don't leave the house unless we're with you.'

'Not at all?' said Declan.

'No, not at all. Even if you want to go to the shops, or a stroll, or anything like that, you just don't leave—okay?'

'Why,' asked Declan.

'Because these people are good,' said Julian. 'And these people will leave you dead and then move on to the next of us.

So, in the meantime, stick closely together. Don't wander off until Siobhan and I can sort this out.'

'But how does it end?' asked Kylie.

'Well, we've got a problem. We don't know how many are in the group. So we're going to have to trap one to find out,' said Julian.

'Trap one,' said Declan. 'But you said this was a hitman. This was—'

'The entire group are not hitmen. Somebody will be a fixer. Somebody will be there to provide backup. Somebody will be there to assist them in the good times.'

'Why does he need help in the good times?' asked Declan.

'Because sometimes you have to come back, mentally. Some of what they do is very dark, Declan.'

Siobhan stood up, went to the window, looked out and then came back again. 'If we need to catch them, if we need to draw one out, then it'll be me. I'm the one they really want. I'll be ready for them.'

'I think that's unwise in some ways,' said Julian.

'I've clearly been the focus of this all along and it's my responsibility to take it on.'

'You never talked about responsibility in the service,' said Julian. 'You never pulled that thread.'

'I'll be bait,' said Siobhan.

'Why? Why you?' said Julian.

'I'll be bait, because I'm the most recognisable. I'm the one they want to come for.'

'But I can do that,' said Julian. 'You can observe them then.'

'No, I'm the one they want. I want you to observe, and I want those two right out of it.'

'I might have an idea how to draw them out of the shadows,'

said Julian. 'The video Alex left of Randolph might be the key. The thing I'm very aware of is, if you're dealing with a group, did Alex offend the group? Did he betray someone? The only thing we knew Alex was working on was Randolph.'

'And Randolph's dead,' said Declan. 'So how do we think that through?'

'We've still got the video,' said Julian. 'We can still raise merry hell with that.'

'What are you suggesting?'

'We put it up there. We let it run. Tell the Fredericks that we're going to broadcast it. We're going to have people coming after us. You see,' said Julian, 'I don't think Alex killed Randolph, but maybe one of the group killed Alex before he could. Randolph would be an expensive mark. I don't know the dynamics of the group, but normally the person who kills takes most of the money. After all, that's the hard bit. That's the bit where you get caught and you're in big trouble.'

'The Fredericks are involved,' said Declan, 'and we're going to rattle their cages?'

'We don't really know much about the other side, do we? Let's see what we can shake up by talking to them,' said Julian. 'See who comes forward and out of the muck.'

'I don't get this,' said Siobhan. 'I'm not good with it.'

'Why? If we don't, we should all just clear out to South America,' said Julian. 'We're going to be out of even the Service safe houses soon.'

'Who do you think could do it then?' asked Siobhan. 'Do you think if we bring it all in front of the Fredericks that they'll suddenly, what, talk to people, put people on us?'

'Somebody's already paid this group to get on us. It might have been the Fredericks. After all, they did want a hold of us.

They know we know stuff about them.'

'But we made peace and we aren't annoying them,' said Siobhan.

'Maybe you should. Maybe that's what's required. We need to bring this all out into the light to find out who did it,' said Julian.

'We could wait,' said Siobhan. 'We could wait and see how this plays out. We're in no hurry. The moment we step outside that door, the moment we go somewhere, we're in danger. We stay here and it's not a problem.'

The group looked at each other nervously, afraid of what was coming, but also determined to get to the end.

Chapter 25

'So how do we do this?' said Siobhan.

'Well, we're going to involve the Fredericks' estate. Then we need to just ask. We need to walk in and talk to them. We need to bring them into it. After all,' said Julian, 'it seems to me that they've got an interest in this. Somebody killed Randolph. They'll want to find them. They'll want to find them and despatch them, this entire group.'

'We'll have to see if they've got the stomach for it, though,' said Siobhan.

'Well, if somebody just killed my brother, and then another brother, I'd probably have the stomach for it,' said Declan.

'People don't always work like that, Declan,' said Kylie. 'Some people would just quit. I mean, these people have everything anyway, don't they? Lots of money, lots of—'

'Lots of clout and family prestige,' said Siobhan. 'They're exactly the type who would want to get even. Part of the reason they came after us was because they thought we were investigating them, and we were going to talk about Randolph. They'd also want to know if we knew anything about Randolph's killer.'

'What if we tell them we might know who the killer is then!'

said Julian.

'That'll bring them in,' said Siobhan. 'Bring them in and keep them guessing. We might use them.'

'I'm not a hundred per cent sure how,' said Julian. 'But we contact them, and we're still seen as being on the ball. We might coax the Fox out for the chickens, then.'

'I don't like that analogy,' said Siobhan. 'I won't be a chicken waiting for the Fox to come in and steal me.'

'Well, let's go out and grab them. The Fox and his people will have tabs on the Fredericks. After all, they killed off at least one—if not possibly two—of the family. So they want to see what they're doing in retaliation. They will want to monitor them. If they do that, they'll see us purporting to know the score and we can bring them out.'

'So, I'm off to the Frederick Estate then,' said Siobhan.

'I'll come with you,' said Julian.

'No. You need to be here in case something happens. You need to look after these two as well,' said Siobhan. 'If the two of us got caught, they won't know what to do. They won't know where to run or how to run. You do. If something happens to me, you get everybody out.'

Julian nodded, but he wasn't happy about the decision. Siobhan went upstairs and dressed for the meeting. She put on a pair of blue jeans, the jumper she liked with the roll neck, and then wrapped it up in a large coat. She turned to Julian as he entered the room.

'Have you got anything?'

'Heat, you mean,' he said. 'I can furnish you with some pistols.'

'No, I'll let them search me. Some knives I can secrete, something I can fight my way out with.'

'Apart from these wonderful fists of yours?'

'Not funny, Julian. I need something; I need something in case I'm trapped.'

'I've got some needles, poison needles you can spit, you remember how to do that don't you?'

Julian produced a small packet of needles. Siobhan took the packet, put it in her pocket, aware that she may need to use them later on.

'You all set?' asked Julian.

'Wish me luck.'

He grabbed her, pulled her close, and kissed her. For a moment, she felt like he would not let go. But she kissed back.

'We get clear of this, then you're out for good,' he said.

'If we get out of it?' she said, looking at him, 'you don't sound sure.'

'If we get out of it,' said Julian. 'I'm not sure at all.'

She held him close. 'I'll get out of it for you.'

* * *

Siobhan was aware that Julian was watching from the window as she drove off, heading for the Frederick estate. They had a smaller estate in Northern Ireland, not as big as the English one, but she knew somebody would be there. After all, the brother had only just died over here. Siobhan approached the gatehouse and was let through. She drove up to the front doors, and a man stepped out.

'Miss Frederick will see you now.'

'Very good,' said Siobhan.

'Your keys, please,' said the man.

Siobhan handed the keys of the car over and a younger man

184

drove it off to park it elsewhere. Siobhan was taken up grey marble steps through two large double entrance doors into a wood-panelled lobby. There followed another wood-panelled corridor before going through what felt like a maze of rooms until she appeared in a large ballroom. In the middle of the ballroom was a table set up and sitting behind it was what looked like a young teenage girl.

'My name is Veronica. I am the daughter of Xavier Frederick. My mother is long departed. The estate is mine.'

'Forgive me for asking, but what age are you?'

'Seventeen,' said the girl. 'But it is mine. And Emma here works for me now.'

Siobhan glanced to her right and saw Emma, who had tricked them so eloquently.

'I think you and I have a common enemy,' said Siobhan.

'I don't see how you work that out. My father told me everything about meeting you. He said you were lucky you had such a faithful lapdog to save you.'

'Lapdogs don't save you. Good men, faithful men, save you,' said Siobhan.

'I would very much like to know who killed my father,' said Veronica. 'I'm assuming it wasn't you, since you're here.'

'When we left your father's company, we disappeared. On hearing of his death, we came back to the office. I was going to come here and try to make peace with him before he died. But somebody beat me to that. I am here with you, not to make peace. But to see if we can be of assistance to each other.'

'Why would you want help from me? My father wanted you dead. Now my father is dead. You turn up and present yourself in front of me. Why? I could just despatch you now like he had wanted to.'

'Even he would have wondered why I was back. You want revenge for whoever killed your father. And it wasn't me,' said Siobhan. 'You want revenge for whoever killed Randolph. And that wasn't me either. Your father and your uncle's killings must weigh heavily on you. I think we can help each other.'

'I think she can,' said Emma, 'if I may say so.'

'If I'd like your advice, I'll ask for it,' said Veronica. 'I am speaking. Siobhan Duffy, you talk about revenge; you talk about who killed my father and my uncle. This is no place to talk about things like that. We shall meet tonight.'

'Are you telling me this isn't secure?'

'Our family has a number of interests, some of which we have to come to at certain times. My father lies in state, behind us. You don't put such a man somewhere secret. He's dead and he's in the family home in this land. We have others coming to see him. So, when we speak, we will speak in private. In the best private place there could be,'

'In public then,' said Siobhan.

'My father would have liked you. It's a pity he wanted to kill you.'

'Where do you want to meet?' asked Siobhan.

'We think Belfast's going to be alive tonight. A lot going on. They've put an enormous wheel in by the city hall. I have always wondered what it would be like to sit in it, especially at night. Gaze at the summer light dimming on the city. Maybe we can meet on it later tonight. Say at seven? It won't be dark then. We should get a good view of everything.'

'Seven o'clock it will be.'

'Come alone,' said Veronica. 'I'll be there. But come alone.'

As Siobhan turned away, Veronica stopped her. 'What is your interest in this case?'

'Your father knew a clicnt's brother. He was found dead with a picture of your uncle in a compromising position. He had a flat and too much money.'

'And that's why you looked at us. Yet you had a close call and you could have walked away. Now you are back. Why?'

'Professional interest,' said Siobhan.

'If we want to work together, you need to be more open than that.'

'Whoever was after your uncle, or whoever was after your father, they're after us now. I don't know why. I would have walked, but I can't, because they're not letting me.'

'Tonight, then,' said Veronica. 'Seems that we have a common enemy.'

Siobhan walked back along the wood-panelled halls and down the grey marble steps, where her car was waiting for her. She got inside and looked around at all the opulence that the estate offered.

Siobhan drove off, making her way back to the safe house. She pulled up after taking a circuitous route to make sure no one was following her. Julian was waiting on the doorstep. She got out, ran over, and he hugged her tight.

'It appears we have a teenage girl now in charge. But she seems to have her head screwed on.'

'Families like that, they train them from young. Train them to think,' said Julian.

'She is thinking. She wouldn't even let me talk there. We're talking tonight in Belfast.'

'In Belfast? She really mustn't trust the people around her.'

'We'll want the four of us on the go though,' said Siobhan. 'We need as many people watching. Hopefully by coming out, we can present myself and Veronica as a target. We might get a Fox following us.'

'We'd best get you prepped up then. You sure you're up for this? There are always the other options,' said Julian.

'The beach?'

'An island beach. The far-off South Seas island beach.'

'What am I going to do sitting around in a bikini all day, soaking up the rays?'

'There's fishing. And besides, you sitting around in a bikini all day doesn't sound that bad to me.'

'If I went—' said Siobhan.

'If you went, you would be restless. You'd be hell to be with. You might go after seeing something through, but not right now,' said Julian.

'I'm sorry,' said Siobhan. 'I keep dragging you back into this. All you want is me. And possibly that bikini.'

'Not to worry. I'm sure it wouldn't fit me. But it's those two I worry about,' said Julian. 'I can look after myself. I'm not sure they can.'

Chapter 26

Belfast was alive. The International Food Market was in town and the streets around City Hall were as crowded as anything. People bustled here and there, getting their sauerkraut. There were breads from all over the world, bites here, there, and everywhere. There was even alcohol of all types on sale. And everyone in Belfast seemed to enjoy themselves, except for Siobhan.

She was dressed in her jeans again, a simple jacket wrapped around her this time. Inside of that jacket was a handgun. She didn't want to use it. She wanted to use the other side of the jacket, which had different items available to her. Items that could render someone unconscious.

The hope was that in meeting out in daylight that someone would come to take her out. How and where she didn't know. One thing she suspected was that the Fredericks had a problem. Two of their number had been dispatched. Was there somebody on the inside feeding out information? Strangely enough, Siobhan hoped so.

She walked towards the city hall, glancing over at the large wheel, set to one side of the building. It would give a cracking view of Belfast as the summer light was only just starting to wane. It was probably the brightest day they'd had in a long while but now the light was fading slightly. Not to a point where the streetlights were required.

Siobhan stepped this way and that, conscious that around her were lots of people she didn't know. As she skipped amongst the stalls, she saw Kylie, not that far off her, but heavily disguised. She looked like an old woman and Siobhan was deeply proud of the makeup and how she'd achieved such an old look with her. Kylie was playing her part, too. The hunched back, the stuttering steps.

Julian was also out and about, as was Declan. They had made themselves up separately and disappeared off before Siobhan could see them. She wanted to avoid any lingering glares at them, anything that would give her or them away. Siobhan had one goal: find the wheel, get on board, and then find Veronica.

Siobhan approached the city hall, walked around the edge of it, and paused occasionally. She was looking for anyone lingering, anyone that looked out of place. All she saw were families laughing, lads out together for a night in the town, women with shopping purchases. Some were laughing as they bought candy floss or tried a morsel of something they didn't really recognise.

The market was a great thing for Belfast. The place was alive; it was busy; it was exciting, but tonight it could be deadly.

Siobhan queued up for the wheel but she couldn't spot her prize. She couldn't see the teenage daughter of Xavier Frederick. In fact, she couldn't see anyone from the household. Instead, there was an obese man beside her. He had earphones in and a bushy beard. His jumper was scruffy and smelly, underneath a well-worn coat. On the other side, a blonde woman stood beside Siobhan. But she seemed to take little notice.

Slowly, the queue moved forward as the wheel turned round, bit by bit. There was nothing for it except to get on board and Siobhan made her way when the pod came round, stepping in along with the man with the earphones and the blonde woman. Also stepping into the pod were two parents with a small child.

They went to one corner of the pod, sitting down and pointing out all the delights of Belfast to the child while Siobhan stood along with the blonde woman. The obese man, teetering about, was obviously struggling to stand. He eventually deposited himself in one seat at the side of the pod. But the blonde woman continued to look over Siobhan's shoulder. Quickly and quietly, Siobhan felt something in her back. The blonde woman whispered to her.

'Apologies, but I'm here to negotiate. Veronica won't be here tonight.'

Siobhan froze. *How did she miss her? How did she miss that woman?* Now, she was up in the pod, trapped away.

'What do you want?' whispered Siobhan.

'Well, I want more than you. Your team's going to gather back with you. We'll gather back at wherever you're holding out. And when we meet, I'll despatch you.'

'Who are you?' Siobhan asked.

'You really didn't get far into this, did you? I'm the Fox. The one who was coming for the chickens. I've come for you.'

The pod continued on its way round, rising to near the top. It stopped for a moment, letting people off down below. The family in the corner with the child couldn't see what was happening and continued to laugh. They pointed out to the child all the vantage points around Belfast.

Siobhan was stuck. If she fought the woman here, it could be a long time before she would subdue her, during which time the family, the child, even this obese man, could be in trouble. Siobhan couldn't enact anything right now.

A hand slipped inside Siobhan's jacket, taking out her gun and slipping it away. The woman smiled.

'You were obviously expecting trouble. Bringing a firearm with you. You're not one for firearms, if I remember right.'

Somebody had done their research clearly and Siobhan wondered if she would get back out of this. She looked around at those in the pod wondering was it worth it, giving it a go. The large man stood up, and he seemed to wander around a bit. The ride moved on, getting past the apex, and came partly down the other side before it stopped again.

They would have to let each person out of their pods one by one, and Siobhan knew she had as long as it took to get down to enact something or she'd be off into the city. She didn't think that the woman was daft enough to cause a scene, but if she ran for it in public, maybe she would kill her. After all, she was a hitwoman. And she would despatch. They were merciless, doing it for the money, never questioning.

"This is good, ja?' said the obese man.

Great, thought Siobhan. *Tourist. That's all I need.*

'Can you tell me? I ask you now, ja? Where ist Samson?'

'I'm sorry, I can't help you,' said the woman, still holding the gun into Siobhan's back.

'No, you're from Belfast, and I think you will understand. Where ist Samson? Samson? And Goliath, yes? Not Delilah, but Goliath. They are big, big for ships. You understand me? They are big for ships.'

The woman looked over at the German man. "I really can't

help you, sir.'

Samson and Goliath were two enormous cranes in the shipyard and could be clearly seen with the ride at its apex.

'Please, you help me.'

The family in front took pity on the tourist. 'It's over there, mate. Look, see the crane?'

'No, no, I don't see properly.'

'Over there.' The pod began to move again, spinning round and the German stumbled. His right hand shot out and hit the hip woman on the side of the neck.

'Oh, I apologise. Pardon. I apologise. You must think me a big oaf. Ya?'

Siobhan felt the gun slip slightly off her back. The Fox was beginning to swoon. Siobhan saw the eyes roll. The obese man slipped an arm underneath, catching the woman as she fell. Siobhan did the same.

'Get the guns,' said a voice. 'Mrs D, get the guns.'

Siobhan stared at the German. It was Declan. How on earth?

Declan tried not to grin, but turned round to the family.

'We have big heights here. She is, oh! How do you say it in English? She is wibbly-wobbly. She is all over this place. Yes? Yes? Too high to see Goliath. Too high for crane. We may sit her down. Quick, we sit her down.'

Siobhan helped Declan sit the woman in one of the seats. It was a remarkable feat, thought Siobhan. Not only was he acting, but he slapped her on the back of the neck and activated some poison. She stared at the hands of Declan and saw a ring that he normally would not have worn.

Brilliant, she thought, *just brilliant, and I never gave the game away because I didn't know his disguise.* When the pod eventually reached the ground, Siobhan let the family get off first, before carrying the woman with Declan. With an arm under each of the woman's arms, they carried her along the streets. Suddenly, a car pulled up beside them. The door was flung open, and an elderly woman stood in front of it.

'Get her in the back.' The voice, however, was young. It was Kylie. Siobhan looked inside the car and saw Julian in the driver's seat.

'Brilliant,' she said, 'just brilliant.'

Declan climbed in first and they lifted the woman in, followed by Siobhan, before all doors of the car slammed shut. They drove off, and Siobhan looked around at the faces next to her. She barely recognised them.

'Next time I want to put on a play, you guys are all in, you hear me?'

'Yah, Mrs D, yah,' said Declan. Kylie shook her head.

Chapter 27

The team arrived back at the safe house. Julian made sure that all the safeties were installed and that they would be undisturbed. Then they set about interrogating the woman they'd brought back with them.

First, they sat her on a chair in the middle of a sitting room. She was tied tight and also gagged so she couldn't speak. Julian and Siobhan took it in turns to make sure they were in the room with her. Her hands were cuffed behind her, and she was frisked, with several weapons being removed.

The Fox stared at them as Siobhan examined her. She was of middling height, her build fairly slender, perfect for disguises. It was always easier to put on weight, to put on a shape than try to reduce it. Her hair was short and cropped, but her eyes were everywhere, watching everything.

'What do we do with her then?' asked Siobhan.

'We need her to talk,' said Julian. 'You may want to send the other two out, if needs be. Although she may talk anyway.'

Siobhan removed the gag around the woman's mouth, brought in a cup of water and let her sip it. She then sat down in front of her, Julian walking behind the woman, with Declan and Kylie sitting on one side.

'Quite a bruised-up little face there,' the woman said to Siobhan. She could only have been in her thirties, but she exuded a confidence, even in this dire situation for her.

'I think you need to talk,' said Siobhan. 'You're not in the best situation.'

'No, yet you need me alive. I've come to kill you; you capture me and you keep me alive. You must need me for a reason.'

'We do indeed,' said Julian. 'I want to know about you, what you've done, and also who you work with.'

'And I do what? Tell you all this and then you despatch me? What would be the point of telling you? Other than to secure an extra half hour of my existence. I could, however, move on. I can pay you off. Pay you not to say anything. Give you a million. I have a million stashed away. Been building up, you see. I don't want to do this for the rest of my life. It's risky as I'm now finding out, but I could pay you. Disappear off to some foreign land.'

'That's a thought,' said Julian. 'Let me discuss it.'

He turned so his back was to the woman. He whispered into Siobhan's ear. 'That's not a good play,' he said. 'Let her out. She's free to kill us, and she will. However, keep her and you never know what we could do with her.'

'I know,' said Siobhan, 'but we'll play with her, see if she'll talk, see if she really knows who we are. Maybe she doesn't, and that's why she's been caught.'

Julian spun round. 'Okay,' he said, 'let's have your name for a start.'

'Oh no, I don't tell you my name.'

'Well, let's call you Susan,' said Julian. 'Makes it a lot easier. Means we're able to converse more quickly.'

'Susan, it is then.'

'So, you work as a hired killer,' said Julian. 'How many people have you killed?'

'Plenty,' Susan said. 'Most have been minor jobs. You don't get that many big contracts.'

'Work alone?' asked Julian.

'Not quite. I did at the start. Then I got myself a middleman. Someone to introduce the clients to me. Or rather, keep them at a distance from me. I've had a couple of them in my time. They're no longer around.'

'Occupational hazard for working with you,' said Siobhan.

'You could say that,' said Susan. 'Sometimes, you just get bored with people. In fairness, a couple of them betrayed me. One rather nice guy I wasn't sure about. You don't take any risks in this business, though.'

'So, you've done most things low level then,' said Julian.

'Well, the thing is that Randolph's family, they were the big ones, weren't they? I mean, you probably heard of me.'

'The Fox.'

'Yes, the Fox.'

'So who else have you despatched?' asked Julian. He looked over at Declan and Kylie. They were tight-lipped in the corner. They'd been told to remain so but he could see that they were nervous about what was happening.

'I despatched Randolph Frederick.'

'How?' asked Julian.

'Well, as you can see, I'm not that unattractive. I needed to get close. Heart attack, they said. It's quite something to bring on a heart attack in the throes of passion, isn't it?'

'I take it you injected him with something? You didn't just burn him out.'

'The problem with Randolph was he thought he owned

197

people. Got people close and then, well, you don't want to know. That was a good payday, though. And the fire afterwards—his brother's death. That was the Fox, too,' she said.

'We're getting confused though,' said Julian. 'You said you used to have people working for you. Who works for you currently? How do you make contact?'

'Doesn't matter,' said the woman. 'I pay you and I run. It doesn't matter. They won't see me again. They'll be too scared to do anything about it.'

'Humour me,' said Julian. 'Tell me how it works.'

'That's the clever bit,' said the woman. 'And I guess I should warn you, especially if I'm on the run, I won't be the only one coming after you.'

'Was the contract on us put out to many people?' asked Julian.

'No. The reason the Fox is so good is there's five of us. That's why they never see us coming. All different. Imagine one minute you see a man. The next minute, the Fox is a woman. How do the police handle that? The Fox becomes a rumour. Five of us. And we just get the details of whom to kill. And then we get paid. You were the latest. Siobhan there, and her team. They said the Fox was killed in Tollymore Forest Park, the body left at the hermitage.

'That was a blow,' said Susan, 'really was—good part of the team—but you move on.'

'Have you recruited anyone else, then?'

'No,' says Susan, 'we don't do that. There'll be another three of us coming after you. I mean it. I'll keep out of the way.'

'No doubt you will,' said Siobhan, 'but we were targeted. Somebody sent us a glitter bomb.'

Susan nearly choked with laughter. 'Never heard of one of them. How does that work then? Send you into a disco frenzy?'

Siobhan was impressed by the woman's cool, cracking jokes at a time like this. Julian was off walking behind her, checking her hands, making sure everything was still in place. They'd been in the company of too many good assassins, too many operatives who could get out of trapped situations. You had to watch for it. Keep it in mind.

'So,' said Siobhan, 'you didn't send a glitter bomb to our offices. You didn't warn us.'

'It wasn't me. Not the Fox's style either, as I said. I've told you everything. Told you how I work. Told you who else is coming after you. So, do we have a deal? If I can get you the million, you can come with me. I store it, it's not in a bank. It's that extra special reserve kept away. Don't trust the bank.'

She's lying with that, thought Siobhan. *There's no way she keeps that amount of money lying around somewhere. Of course she'd use a bank. But it wouldn't be a normal one. It'd be one of the special ones, or a Swiss one with a number.* Siobhan didn't trust her. 'We'll think about it. You'll stay here.'

'Wherever here is,' says Susan.

'You don't seriously expect us to show you where you are.'

Siobhan stood up, eyed the woman and left the room. She indicated for Declan and Kylie to follow her out, which they dutifully did so. Julian was last, switching off the lights in the room. Outside on a small screen was an image of the room, but with an infrared night vision picture showing. Julian could see the woman clearly, although she couldn't see anything.

'What do you want to do?' said Julian.

'Maybe we could take her money,' said Declan, 'and we could

199

pay off the other ones that come. Maybe we could pay them all off.'

'You don't get their reputation,' said Siobhan, 'by paying off people and running. She's not genuine, Declan. We're letting her play us for saps, but she's not genuine.'

'I think she's genuine in what she's saying, though. She's boasting, telling us how she's killed,' said Julian. 'I think there may be more coming after us.'

'Well, if that's the case, we need to draw more out again,' said Siobhan. 'As if the last one wasn't bad enough.'

'How do we do it, then?'

'Well, last time,' says Siobhan, 'we went to Veronica. Somebody in there is clearly working for them. Somebody close to Veronica. It would be good for her to know, so I'm sure she'll play along.'

'And what?' said Julian. 'We just keep playing this game? We just keep going and going?'

'That's what we have to do,' said Siobhan. 'If we don't, we're stumped. They'll come for us. They'll find us at some point.'

'We could run,' said Julian. 'Go away, far side of the world. We can have a decent life. Stay quiet, stay low. We'd have each other,' said Julian. 'Declan here would have Kylie. Kylie would have Declan.'

'I'd have to leave everyone then,' said Declan.

'Yes, we would,' said Julian. 'We would.'

'Not that easy for us,' said Kylie. 'You have got no family, friends. You came from a place where you might have to run one day. You've lived with that your whole life.'

'We're not doing that,' said Siobhan. 'I won't run with something over my head for the rest of my life. And I won't give up here. I came back here because this is where I want to be. Here with you,' she said to Julian. 'I can't ask these two to give up their families.'

Julian turned away. 'You know this could end up really bad,' said Julian.

'I know,' said Siobhan. 'But I trust in you and I trust in us. We can do this. We need to make sure she's secure, though.'

'I will do, and I need to teach you a few things about this house.'

Chapter 28

It was a bright morning when Siobhan drove into the Fredericks estate again, asking for an audience with Veronica. She was advised that the woman was unavailable because she was recovering from being out late the previous night. Siobhan almost laughed because she hadn't slept since the previous night. She insisted so hard that Veronica be told of her arrival that the doorman disappeared off, leaving Siobhan inside in the lobby.

She stared around, looking at the opulence, amazed at the wooden decor. There were a few large pictures which looked fairly modern but done in an older style. One was of Veronica; the other was Randolph. Xavier was on the opposite wall. Veronica would play along—of course, she would.

'The lady will see you now. Follow me,' said the doorman. He took Siobhan through a wooden panel, into what looked like a secret corridor, which opened up into a small breakfast room. Sitting at a table wrapped up in an elegant dressing gown was Veronica.

'Oh, good morning. Missed you last night.'

'I don't think you did. I think someone delayed you.'

'That's true. I was held back for a phone call. I think I was maybe half an hour late. When we arrived, you weren't there.'

'I had been there. Someone made an attempt on my life. We're holding them but don't let that get out.'

'So why are you back here?'

'The thing is, Veronica, somebody here is leaking information. I realised that last night. It's not you. You've lost too much. It's somebody else. Betrayed your father and your uncle.'

Siobhan watched the woman's fist clench. 'Do you know who?'

'I have my suspicions. However, I'll keep them at the moment.'

'Why?' asked Veronica.

'Is this room safe?' asked Siobhan.

'Yes.'

Siobhan walked up to her, sat down beside her, and pulled out a small pad of paper from inside her coat pocket. She wrote with a pen. 'I don't trust any room,' the note said. 'I believe Emma may be the one.'

Veronica took the pen off Siobhan and wrote 'Why?'

Siobhan wrote, 'Because she wants money. She wants in with the big leagues. Somewhere where she can earn this money repeatedly. I don't think she's earning much from you. Not compared to what she could earn from them.'

The pen was taken over again. 'The Fox?'

Siobhan took the pen back. 'The Fox is several people. I have one, but I need the rest. I am going to be meeting you at the Carrick-a-Rede rope bridge tonight. Make sure you look to go, and if nobody stops you, find a reason for things to go wrong timing wise. Blow the tyre on the car, or something. But we will meet there at midnight. Make sure that people close to you know.'

'Seeing as we missed last time,' said Veronica, out loud. 'We should meet up again,'

'Good idea,' said Siobhan, 'but well out of the way, not crowded like Belfast.'

'Carrick-a-Rede,' said the woman, 'the rope bridge at Carrick-a-Rede. How about that?'

Siobhan finished tucking her pad of paper and pen back inside her jacket,

'I shall see you there at midnight. We have plenty to discuss,' said Siobhan. She went to turn, but Veronica held up her hand. She rang a little bell, and the same doorman who had shown her in took Siobhan back down the secret corridor and back out to the lobby. Outside the building, Siobhan's car was brought round. She drove off back to the safe house.

Siobhan slept for most of the day, only taking her turn to watch the prisoner. Even though the room was secure, Julian said he wanted someone to watch from the outside. There were plenty of things within the room that could incapacitate and take out their suspect if needed though.

'Best if I have you with me,' said Siobhan, 'when we go to Carrick-a-Rede. How are we going to run this here? Are you happy to leave Declan in charge?'

'We leave Declan and Kylie together,' said Julian. 'We'll drug our captive, so she'll be flat out the whole time we're away. But in case she does wake up, we have briefed them on things they can do. She shouldn't get out of the room, and they'll be here to watch her. If she gets active, we'll soon knock her out again. We can gas the room.'

'I do like this room,' said Siobhan. 'I like this house. We should have used it before.'

'There aren't many houses like this,' said Julian. 'But once it's compromised, it's compromised. It took time to put this in place. Weekends on my own, and with contractors I truly trusted.'

'It's working out for us,' she said and disappeared off to get ready for the evening.

Julian and Siobhan drove from Belfast up to the north coast and arrived at the car park for the Carrick-a-Rede rope bridge. There was a delightful walk down to it, and Julian drove off in the car, having deposited Siobhan. He quickly drove away, telling Siobhan that he would park up and then follow her closely.

Siobhan walked along in a long coat as if she was out for a summer's evening. The view from the path was exquisite, the blue water on her left-hand side with the fresh sea smell. There was the crunch of gravel beneath her feet. She wished she could bring Julian along here. Maybe she would, once this was all sorted.

That was good. You had to keep it in your head that it would all get sorted. Of course it would.

Siobhan would cross the bridge tonight. They had closed it up. After all, they didn't want anyone messing around on it. It was a rope bridge, with greater safety features these days, but still a daunting bridge for the uninitiated.

When Siobhan got closer, she thought about what she was to do. When she went to the isle on the other side of the bridge, she would be trapped. There was no easy way off, except back over the bridge. Going down to the water required a quick trip, off a cliff edge with no guarantee you'd hit the water.

Siobhan reached the end of the path and went down some stone steps, reaching the steeper, small section of path that

205

led to the start of the bridge. She remembered crossing the old bridge back in the day when it looked a lot scarier. These days, it was safer; there was a lot around it, more controlled. Back in the day, when you ran across it, it swung and bounced. It still did these days, but not to the same degree. She felt now there were more ropes to hang on to, less chance of you disappearing through it.

She clambered up and over the guard stopping people from going through to the bridge. She then tiptoed across it, stopping momentarily in the middle, looking down at the dizzying water below, before continuing across. Behind her, she thought she heard a noise.

Once, on the far side of the isle, Siobhan walked around and then dropped to the ground, taking herself out of sight. Looking back, she saw a figure emerging, leaving the end of the bridge towards her. But she also saw one further back. Two figures? Had Veronica mistimed—here when she shouldn't be?

Siobhan walked now, standing up, so she could be seen to the furthest point of the isle away from the bridge. She sat down in the grass, looking out to the dark sea beyond.

They approach quietly, she thought, *very quietly*. She turned to see the first figure, their head just emerging over the top of the isle. And then they couped sideways, falling to the ground. Siobhan turned back, looking out to sea. A bead of sweat trickled down her face. She waited. Was that the sound of someone coming off the bridge?

Siobhan listened carefully. Amongst the night noises, amongst the occasional crash of the sea waves, she could hear them getting closer. They'd be very close soon.

'Siobhan Duffy,' said a voice. Siobhan stood up, slowly

turned around.

'Who are you?' she asked.

'Nothing personal,' said a man's voice. 'It's just business.'

She saw the gun rise up, the silencer on the end, and then the man fell to one side. She strode over, took the gun out of his hand, then checked the other fallen pursuer. Having swept him for weapons, she turned to see someone else now get up from the grass on the aisle.

'Any others?' asked Siobhan.

'Went rather well, didn't it?' said Julian. 'No others. Who'd have thought I could have beat you round and across?'

'You must be exhausted.'

'You could say that. Good job they didn't take you out on the path.'

'They needed to know I was on my own,' said Siobhan. 'Needed to make sure that Veronica wasn't waiting. Apparently, she had a problem.'

'You've spoken to her,' said Julian.

'No. I told her if someone didn't make one for her, she was to make one for herself.'

Siobhan walked over to Julian, put her arms around him, and kissed him. She stood holding his hand. 'We should have run,' she said. 'We should have run.'

'One to go, tough,' said Julian. 'One to go.'

'And if we get them, what do we do with them?' asked Siobhan. 'I'm not for taking them out somewhere and just despatching them. It's not me, I mean,'

'Well, they're wanted for quite a few murders. You could give them to Veronica.'

'Can't be sure then, though. What does she do with them? And if she's got somebody inside an organisation working for them, they'd have to stand there and watch them being despatched. They could react before their deaths.'

'We could always go to the Service. That would be interesting. The Service would be keen to talk to them. They'd sort them.'

'I suppose. One more though. We've also got a bit of work to do.'

'Do you think anybody's ever carried someone over their shoulder across that bridge?' asked Julian. She wouldn't look at it. It swung when she walked across. It bounced and was far from her favourite thing to do. And now she'd do it with someone over her shoulder.

'You couldn't have thought of somewhere else?' said Julian. 'Somewhere a bit nearer a car park?'

Siobhan laughed. 'Come on,' she said. 'We'd best get done and get out of here. Get these two back. As long as Kylie and Declan are okay. I wasn't happy leaving that woman with them.'

'That house is good,' said Julian. 'they'll be fine, trust me. They'll be fine.'

Chapter 29

A car rolled into the driveway and parked up behind the trees that hid it from the road. Julian got out and opened up the boot where two prone hitmen were lying on top of each other. Julian had drugged them to make sure they wouldn't wake up. He was now ready to lift them and put them inside. As Siobhan got out of the car, Kylie came running outside of the house.

'He's gone. I told him not to go. I told him to wait for you. But he's gone.'

'Declan?' said Siobhan. 'What do you mean, he's gone?'

'He got a call. Wouldn't wait. He wouldn't wait, said he had to be there. Had to protect them. Had to—'

Kylie was in a tizzy now, and Siobhan grabbed her shoulders. 'Calm down,' she said. 'Can't do anything when you're like this. I need to understand what's happened. Calm down.'

Kylie continued to blurt out.

'We're outside,' said Julian. 'Inside. Get her inside now.'

But Kylie was starting to lose it. The words were coming thick and fast. Siobhan slapped Kylie hard across the face. She stopped suddenly, looking petrified at Siobhan. She let Julian disappear to check on the prisoner and took Kylie into the living room. Sitting her down on the sofa, Siobhan placed herself opposite and held Kylie's hands. 'Tell me—Declan, where's he gone?'

'He's gone to his folks. He got a call.'

'What phone?'

'His mobile.'

'His mobile is meant to be off,' said Siobhan. 'You're not meant to have mobiles on in here. That's the whole point.'

'He put it on to check. Wanted to make sure they were all right.'

'He should have told me,' said Siobhan, 'if he was worried about them; we'd check up on them. Julian could have put people on them. Now someone might have Declan.'

'What's up?' said Julian.

'Declan put on his mobile. Message came through from his parents.'

'His mum said there was something unusual round the house,' said Kylie. 'So Declan took off. It was a couple of hours ago. Ten, eleven? Just after, I think.'

'And they knew we were going to be out,' said Julian. 'Don't rush there.'

'Of course, we've got to rush there,' said Kylie. 'Declan could be in trouble; his parents could be in trouble,'

'Declan could be dead,' said Siobhan. Kylie looked at her, mouth open.

'Don't say that.'

'Kylie, right now, we have to think about the right step. If we rush over there, Declan could be dead and we could walk into a trap meant for us. So, we won't rush there. He could also be alive, because you and Declan, you're not the ones they really want.'

'We've also got people here to look after. I'm not happy about both of us disappearing off. I can't leave Kylie here,' said Julian. 'Not the state she's in to look after the three in here.'

'No,' said Siobhan. 'You're right, we can't. Kylie, you need to calm down. You need to pull yourself together. Hopefully, Declan's okay. But if he is, we need to work out how we're going to help him out of the situation he may be in.'

'He might just be at his parents'. It might be nothing,' Kylie said.

'And the hysterics outside were because you thought that?' said Siobhan. Kylie leant forward, tears rushing from her eyes, and cried on Siobhan's shoulder. Holding his hand up, Julian indicated Siobhan should stay with her.

He whispered, 'She needs to let it out.' He turned, disappeared back out to the front of the house, and Siobhan heard him shifting their new captives into the room of the other prisoner.

'Do you need any help?' she asked, when he passed by the door again.

'I've got this bit,' he said.

It took a good five minutes before Kylie lifted her head back up off Siobhan's shoulder. She sniffed. 'I'm okay,' she said, 'I'm okay; we'll do this.'

Siobhan told her to get a drink, and then sought Julian, who was putting the last touches to the captives in the other room. When he stepped outside to Siobhan, he had a worried look on his face.

'Do you think he's dead?' asked Siobhan.

'I hope not,' said Julian. 'I mean, why just him? They did it because they knew we were out. Then he ran. They knew we wouldn't be there. They'll have captured him. They'll either show him to us by giving us a body or they'll expect us to come for him. If they expect us to come for him—'

'—They'll be waiting.'

'Do you want me to go?' said Julian.

'No. I'll go with Kylie. They don't know we're back. Kylie's the one they know won't have gone with us. They know the kids are amateurs. That's why they've gone through Declan. I could get Kylie to approach the door on her own.'

'That's risky. You could be sending her to her death.'

'I know. I'll call it when I'm there. You need to stay here with this lot,' said Siobhan.

'And if he's dead?'

'Let's see how much of a group they are. See how much they care for each other.'

'And if they don't?' said Julian.

'There'll be three less of them to worry about.'

Siobhan turned away, anger rising inside of her. They took Declan. She went into the kitchen, found Kylie, and told her to come with her. As she was about to get out the door, she felt her arm being grabbed by Julian. He pulled her close, and kissed her long and deep.

'It's like you aren't expecting me to come back,' she said.

'Be clever,' he said. 'Don't rush in. Think of your service days. Take Declan out of the equation. I know you're fond of him. We all are. We need to solve the issue, not simply think about him. Treat him like a hostage.'

'How long will you give me before you come after?'

'How long do you need?' asked Julian.

Siobhan looked at her watch. It was nearly four in the morning. She went to get into the car and realised that Julian had already been there. Sitting on the seat was a handgun. She secreted it inside of her jacket before Kylie got in. She wouldn't arm Kylie—the last thing she would do. As they pulled out of the driveway, she saw Julian watching them in the darkness of the front porch.

The drive out towards Declan's was one that seemed like an age. Siobhan had options running through her head, drills and preparations, the way she should think about this, the way she should deal with it. Julian was right, she had to be cold; she had to be exacting.

'It's just round here, isn't it?'

Declan's parents lived on the edge of a modest estate. It was quiet at the moment, being very late. As they drove past the house, there was a light on in the front room. Someone was there. Siobhan could also see a light upstairs.

Siobhan parked up at the end of the street.

'What do we do?' asked Kylie. 'Do we just bang the door and find out if he's okay? Maybe we could text him. I could text him and—'

'We don't text him. We don't let them know what's coming. I want them to think that Julian and I are not back. Whoever has him needs to believe that. Anything you're going to do, you're going to do off your own bat. And because of that, it will be very amateurish. You're going to hope for the best.'

'What are you suggesting?'

Siobhan looked up and down the road. As she did so, she saw a young lad on a moped, pulling into a house. He had a large pannier on the back of his bike with the logo of a pizza company on it. Clearly, he was returning home after a hard night's delivering.

She watched him undo the rear pannier, and lift out a couple of pizzas. Presumably the leftovers from work that he was now going to have before going to bed.

'Say you're hungry,' said Siobhan. 'Let's say you've made your way round.'

'And do what?' asked Kylie.

A plan was formulating in Siobhan's head. 'I think it's time for you to get some pizza. I'm sure the family will be hungry.'

Chapter 30

Kylie was shaking as she approached the door. She fought back some tears, tried to make herself look half-presentable, and then rang the doorbell. Declan's family lived in a detached house, but it wasn't a large one. The front had a small porch with a garden before it, and a driveway running down the side, with a garage beyond. The rear garden was also small and backed on to various other gardens in the estate.

The morning was just about to come up, the dark of the night giving way to a twilight at first, as the sun hadn't truly broken the horizon. The door opened and Declan's mum stood there. Kylie looked at her. The woman's face was full of worry, but she was trying to smile.

'Kylie,' she said, 'why don't you come in? What are you doing here at this time of the morning?'

'Well, I wanted to check up that Declan was okay. I couldn't wait for the others. I needed to know he was all right.'

'Come in,' said the woman. Kylie stepped forward. As soon as she did, she was grabbed, pulled, and spun into the front living room. She saw Declan sitting down on the sofa, went to run for him and felt her arm being pulled again. Kylie was pushed onto a sofa. A man stood before her with a gun in his hand. There was no mask. Kylie realised that meant something bad.

'Where's the other two?' the man asked roughly. He stepped forward, his hand going to Kylie's throat. Declan went to move, but the gun was suddenly pointed at him. 'Where's the other two?' said the man, squeezing her throat.

'Not back!' said Kylie, shaking. She didn't have to put that on. It was no act.

'And you, Mum, you sit down.' Kylie looked over and saw Declan's dad sitting on the other side of the room. 'Well, this is good. We'll maybe get you to call them.'

'She wouldn't allow us to use mobiles.'

'You could call them from here. In a bit,' he said. 'In fact, we might want them to think it's all okay for when they come back. Come round to pick you up.'

'I've ordered pizza,' said Kylie suddenly.

'What do you mean you've ordered pizza?' said the man.

'I thought they're going to be hungry and worried, so I ordered pizza.'

'You cannot be serious,' said the man. 'Pizza. You need to cancel the pizza.'

'I can try,' said Kylie.

'You'd better phone them,' said the man.

'I need to, to call. I need to use the house phone,' said Kylie.

'Don't screw up,' said the man. The phone was brought to Kylie, and she sat on the sofa as she pressed some buttons. On the other end of the line, she was advised that the pizza shop was now closed, and they'd be taking orders again from twelve o'clock the next day. But Kylie said, 'Oh right, really? Okay, well, thank you.'

She put the phone down. The hitman looked at her. 'What?'

'It's left already. He's dropping it here on his way home because it's so late.'

The hitman obviously wasn't happy. 'You're going to have to answer the door when he comes, okay? No funny business, no mucking about.'

The man turned and picked up a drink. There was a tumbler full of a clear liquid, possibly vodka, for all that Kylie knew. He dropped it down his throat, then ordered Declan's father to get him some more. Declan's father came back in with what indeed was Russian vodka, and then the man drank some more.

As they sat waiting, the doorbell went, and the man showed that Kylie should get the door. He walked over behind her, staying out of sight, gun pointed. Kylie opened the door to see a pizza there and a young boy holding it. She pressed forward, reaching for the pizza. 'Nice and easy,' came a whisper from the back. Kylie took the cold pizza, wondering where Siobhan was exactly.

* * *

Siobhan approached their house through the rear garden of the neighbours of Declan's parents. She tried to be quiet, timing her arrival with when the pizza man turned up at the front door. Quickly, she stole forward and took out a set of keys that Kylie had given her.

She thanked God that the pair of them were close enough now that they had actually swapped keys. For this was her way of entry. As long as nothing was bolted. She used her key, undid the back door, and opened it slowly.

She could hear voices at the front. Soon enough, Kylie was on the move to collect the pizza at the front door. Siobhan crept in through a small dining room and opened the door that led into the lounge. She saw Declan's face. He nearly jumped up, but she put her hand up, showing he should stay in his place. A finger went over her lips.

She pointed at Declan's mother and father to stay seated. There was a tumbler of vodka. She indicated the hitman, whose back was still inside the room, hanging on the door that led out to the hall where he could watch Kylie taking the pizza. Pointing at the drink, which had a bottle of vodka sitting beside it, she indicated a question, asking if this was the hitman's. Declan nodded, and carefully Siobhan stole forward.

She dropped the contents of a capsule inside of it, and slowly made her way back out, closing the door, just as she heard the hitman about to come back in. Siobhan made her way round into the hall. The door was still ajar. She took out the gun from inside her coat, just in case anything went wrong.

'You can eat your damn pizza,' said the hitman. 'Guess we're going to have another while to wait until they arrive. We'll give it to the morning. By that point, they should come looking for you. Especially, if they don't know you're back there. But the four of you will not move. You're going to stay in the seat you're in. Eat your pizza.'

'What if I need the toilet?' asked Declan.

'You can shit in your pants. All right, sunshine? You sit there!'

This man was a lot less eloquent than the woman held back at the safe house. Siobhan waited for him to drink. She heard the bottle being undone, the liquid being dropped in, and she hoped he hadn't started a fresh glass. Instead, when she glanced round the corner, he was filling up the one she had dropped the liquid into. He dropped a full tumbler full, before turning back to Declan.

'I hope your old man's got enough drink here for me. I'll not be happy. Keeps me calm, you see. Keeps me rigid. Nice and calm. Nothing happens then. Don't get a drink, I get edgy. You don't know what I'll do. You don't know who I'll do it to. Understand me? You understand me, sunshine?'

'I do,' said Declan quietly. He wasn't rising to the bait, trying to be a hero, which was good. Neither was he looking at the drink, unlike Kylie.

'What are you looking at?' the man suddenly said to her.

'Nothing. Just going to eat my pizza.' Kylie leaned forward to grab the box that she'd placed on the floor. 'Do you mind if I get up and hand it to the others?'

Good girl, thought Siobhan. *Keep it in the moment. Keep them thinking that you've got other priorities.*

'Slowly,' said the man.

Kylie opened the box and walked round, handing a piece of pizza to Declan. Another one to his mum, then to his father before sitting back down, the hitman watching her closely.

'Not a bad little filly, are you? Shame to kill you.'

Siobhan could see Kylie shake but the man turned round and drained the rest of his tumbler. 'That's the problem with you guys. You're too trusting. Don't think. You don't—' He swayed slightly. 'What?' There was another moment. And then the tumbler fell from his hand. 'You bastard!' he said, his head suddenly spinning towards Declan's father.

As he hit the ground, Siobhan stepped in and took the gun away from him. She checked his vitals as he lay there. She placed a knee on his chest, her own gun pointing at his heart. And only when she was satisfied he was out cold, did she look up.

'Mr and Mrs Declan. Apologies for the intrusion. It's wonderful to meet you at last. Siobhan Duffy. Declan may have mentioned me.'

Chapter 31

Siobhan was ecstatic. All four hitmen were in the safe house. Declan was back. Kylie was back. The team was safe. All they had to do now was to work out what to do with the hitmen. She looked at the screen, the four of them, looking green through the night vision as they sat in the darkened room. Julian was beside her.

'I don't think we bring Declan and Kylie into this. I think we send them to bed. They're probably exhausted.'

'*They're* exhausted?!' said Siobhan. 'All I want to do is take you upstairs and cuddle up.'

'Well, that sounds good,' said Julian.

'Yeah, I'm going to sleep,' said Siobhan. 'I may not show it, but my nerves are shot through.'

Julian flicked on the lights for the room the hit men were held in before opening the door and watching them as they blinked, their eyes trying to adjust to the sudden illumination. He would be a blur to them at first, but they would soon focus properly. Siobhan followed him in, the heels of her boots clipping across the floor.

Julian pulled up a chair, grabbed one for Siobhan, and they sat looking at their four hitmen.

'So what do we do with you lot? You've got a contact. Someone that knows all of you,' said Julian. 'Somebody that sets up all the details. I'm thinking it might be somebody in the employ of Veronica. A certain woman there. Does anybody want to enlighten me? Because I'm thinking it might be her. I think I'm going to hand you over to the police.'

The last man that they captured shook his head. 'You can hand us over to the police. What have you got? I was in a house. You drugged me.'

'We drugged you, but you took hostages. People. You had the gun. You had—'

'But I have killed nobody and I have done little. I can sit my time out. I can probably escape. You can't pin anything on me, other than that. And even that, you're going to have to answer your own questions. You were carrying a gun for a start.'

Siobhan looked at Julian. 'It's too messy.'

'What's your name?' asked Julian.

The man didn't say anything. 'Right, then,' Julian said, pointing to him. 'you're Mike. Beside you, there's Dave.' Julian pointed to the man who had been shot down by his colleague. 'And you are Jim. Jim the Betrayer. Well, yourselves and Susan here, might not be prime candidates for the police. But I know other people. I used to be in the Service. Siobhan used to be Service. That's where you made your mistake. You weren't playing with amateurs here. The two kids with us, they're amateurs. You guys aren't. And I've still got friends in the Service. Yes, they don't like us that much. But to hand over the Fox . . .'

Mike looked at him. 'No. I want nothing to do with the Service. They'll just use us.'

'Oh, I can get you to some good people in the Service. You

222

really won't be seen again. You'll be alive but you'll be used for many dubious actions. Maybe they'll have the trainees come in and try to extract information from you. Maybe they'll haul you up to live the rest of your life—half-starved, alone. Driven mad by the loneliness.'

'Look,' said Dave. 'We don't want that. What do you need to know? We can sort this out.'

'We can, can't we?' said Jim, looking at his others.

'Yes,' said Susan. 'We can make a deal. I've already offered you a deal anyway. Have you considered mine?'

Mike looked along the line. 'You let me depart and I'll give a million to forget all of this. Dump this lot in.'

Julian laughed. 'No honour among thieves, eh?' he said. He stood up and walked about.

'I'll offer you a million, too,' said Dave.

'I can get a million for you,' said Jim.

'Well, it's intriguing, everyone,' Julian said. 'But the one thing that bothers me is, there's a contact maker out there. Someone who makes the contacts. Someone that's been dealing with somebody in Veronica's outfit. You see, she's been very helpful to Siobhan here. And we'd like to pay Veronica back.'

'Emma,' said Mike. 'Emma's the one she wants. Emma's been double-playing her all along. Emma's why we knew where you were.'

'Thought so. And Emma's dealing with you? You're the guy. You're the guy making the contacts. That right?'

'Yes. Listen,' said Mike. 'I was the one that set it all up. I was the one that brought them in. No one knows each other, except me, and even I don't know their real names. I just knew they were good; they were up and coming. So I linked through with their contacts, the people who they used to speak to the

223

outside world. Those people are all dead now, and now they all deal through me.'

'It was clever,' said Siobhan. 'Who's the Fox? Is it a man? What size of man, who knows? Look at you, you're all different. You've even got a woman involved, because the Fox is now a woman at times. Well it couldn't have been the Fox, could it? It couldn't have been since it's a woman. But then, the soft kills, the ones where you lull a man in, you have someone then, fair play!'

'I'll give you a million each,' Mike said. 'Think about it. Four million. Four million, you'll be clear. We'll be clear.'

'Got a problem though,' said Julian. 'You don't know these guys, do you? You played a clever trick, but you don't know them.'

'What do you mean?'

'You knew from your contact, Emma, that Siobhan was going to the big wheel to meet Veronica. The job was put up. Susan here took it. We captured Susan. You then heard we were going to Carrick-a-Rede. So you played it clever, you put it up and the other two went for it, and you let them both go. That was the best of it. I think Dave's very lucky that Jim just didn't kill him, but then again Jim was using the tranks because he wanted Siobhan to then bring me out. However, you had disappeared off. They got captured, and because you didn't trust us, you went after Declan because you knew we were away. Smart play, Mike.'

'But there's another problem. One of you is dead,' said Siobhan. 'Alex. Alex died in the hermitage. The Fox. Now the Fredericks all knew it was the Fox. The rumour was the Fox had died, and then the Fox came back. Because they didn't know there were several of you. We only found that out later.

So, one of you,' said Siobhan, 'must have killed Alex.'

'Is that his real name?' said Susan. 'I found the flat. I got his surname. He was Samuels. I found out his surname, got old former colleagues to talk, ones that Mike didn't kill off. Friends of the ones he did,' said Susan. 'Found the flat, followed him, dispatched him,'

'Markham Seafoods—used them in the past, haven't you?' said Siobhan.

'They were the ones who found Alex for me,' said Susan; 'said he was in the flat and I tailed him. Then I killed him.'

'You don't know any of the others, though, do you?' said Siobhan.

'Not telling. I'll give you a million. I'll give you more than a million if you despatch this lot and let me go. Dump them into the Service. I'll get out of here. Nobody knows anything about me. I'll be clear and I'll be clean.'

'You might not understand something about me,' said Siobhan, standing up. She began to walk in front of them. 'I came back here to my home. Troubles were over. The place was lifting itself, getting back on its feet. And yeah, we all know it's not perfect. It'll take generations before all that nonsense sorts itself out. But you know what? This is where I want to be.

'And then somebody killed one of my friends. I got involved with something deeper. And there were murders. Now there's you lot. Everywhere I look, it's not good. Other things below the surface. But I told myself I'm doing a job. And I always did a job. Even when I worked for the service. And I see my jobs through to the end. Julian, here, will tell you. I don't back down. It's my problem. I don't quit. I don't want to lose. I want to do what I was called to do.

225

'So that's what we're going to do. Alex had a brother. And his brother came to me. Wanted me to find out what had happened to Alex. Wanted to know why he was getting half a million pounds from him in his inheritance. Otherwise, I wouldn't be involved.'

'Who put the money out on us?' asked Julian. 'It's the thing I'm not getting. Who did that?'

'I'm not sure the Service liked you,' said Mike. 'The one who came to my contact said it was Service. Told us to carry it out. Paid us well. Or at least paid a good bit up front. I haven't got the other bit yet; I don't think I will get it.'

'No,' said Julian, 'you won't. Can I have moment, please?' he said to Siobhan. They stepped out of the room. Julian switched off the room's lights.

'The service,' he said. 'You buy that?'

'Well, we've pissed them off enough,' said Siobhan. 'You?'

'But Declan and Kylie? The Service? You and me? Well, yeah, if they want us silenced. That might be something that came up in the past, but we don't cry about it that often, you and me.'

'Something we're going to have to look into then,' said Siobhan. 'But we've got them here. Maybe we'll dump them to the Service, anyway. Maybe that'll get them off our backs, whatever it is.'

'I don't think it's the Service,' said Julian. 'Maybe we should wait.'

'We can wait, but I'm bringing Kieran in to see them. And then we can contact the Service. We can make sure everything's all right, and if it's not, we'll sort it. Just want this to be over,' said Siobhan.

'Be thorough,' said Julian. 'Don't rush.'

'I'm not rushing, it's just that . . .'

'What?' asked Julian.

'Declan's family. Declan. When you're in a foreign field, when you're somewhere else, an innocent dies. Well, it's not nice; it's not good, but you don't know them. You know? Declan's parents could have died on this one.'

'Yeah,' said Julian. 'I don't want to say I told you so, but—'

'You said walk away. You said walk away,' said Siobhan. 'My big stubborn head, my desire, kept me going. And then we got to a point where we couldn't walk away. I know, and you're right. And I should listen to you, but we'll solve this, and then we'll get out.'

'Make contact with Kieran then. Let's get that done and dispose of this four to whoever. Make sure we're clear of the Service, and say goodbye to working with this sort of nonsense.'

'Yeah. That's it,' said Siobhan. 'It's a good idea.'

Chapter 32

Siobhan pulled the car over at the kerbside, and the door of the passenger seat opened. Kieran stepped into the car. He had a long coat on and seemed somewhat nervous.

'You said you've done it,' he said. 'You've really done it,'

'I've truly done it,' said Siobhan.

'It's a kind of a relief,' said Kieran, 'all this time, wondering. Are you telling me he was a hitman?'

'He was the Fox. The name's not well known in public circles, but it's well known in the circles of people who try to hunt down such criminals. It's why he had all the money; why he lived in the posh flat. You never suspected?'

'We didn't know each other that well. He hid it from everybody else, too, I take it. It's crazy though, and these guys, you'd think one of them killed him?'

'I know one of them killed him. You see, there was a contract taken out on him. She didn't know at the time who he was. All she had was a name, a surname, found the flat, used some other people to scope it out and then, yeah, follow them one day. Set up a meet in the hermitage. Killed him there.'

'He wasn't that good though, was he?'

'No,' said Siobhan. 'He fell for it. She was able to find him. There was a group of five of them who were the Fox. I don't think she knew who he was. But she knew he was somebody. It's only afterwards, rumours of the Fox dying spread. She wasn't going to tell anybody. She'd killed one of her own. Somebody must have set it up,' said Siobhan. 'One of them. Maybe he was taking too much business. Maybe he was sloppy. I don't know. We've got them to talk to a certain degree, but they're not telling us everything.'

'I'm not sure if I want to meet them,' said Kieran. Siobhan could see his hands shaking.

'It'll be okay. They're completely restrained and won't speak unless we ask them to. They're not being held by the police; they're being held by us. And afterwards, they'll go off to people who, well, know how to handle these people. I just wanted you to have time to look at who killed him. After today, you'll not see them again. Ever!'

'I guess I can live with that,' said Kieran. She drove the car off into the country to the safe house. Parking up outside, she saw Declan and Kylie waiting at the front door.

'Your whole team here?'

'Yes, Kieran. Julian's inside with them at the moment. I'll take you in. He has certain protocols, Julian. We used to work in the secret Service. But you're with me, so don't worry. We'll get you in. We'll get you in front of them. You can talk to them.'

Siobhan smiled at Kylie and Declan as she passed, whispering it was nearly over. She led Kieran into the house and into the room where the four hitmen were being held. Julian was already inside and Siobhan pressed the intercom, giving a code. It was a safeguard, just to make sure that Julian was okay

229

and not under duress. And to check neither was she.

Julian had a control pad inside and effectively ran everything within the room. He pressed a button, and the door could open. Siobhan marched in with Declan and Kylie, who sat in the corner. Kieran, she brought to stand in front of the four hitmen.

'We don't know their names. Susan, Mike, Dave, and Jim though, is what we're using. Mike here is the man who sets everything up. He brought them all together. So, at some point, he enticed Alex in. Though Alex was a hitman before that, Kieran. Susan there is the one who killed him.'

Kieran stared at her.

'It was nothing personal. Just a job.'

'Who gave you that job?'

'Must have been Mike. I got it through a communication,' said Susan.

'So why did you tell her to kill him, Mike? Who told you?'

'Nobody told me,' said Mike. 'No one. I was a bit shocked when Alex died.'

'Had you met my brother? Had you met him when you first took him on?'

'I never knew any names. They were good hitmen. They were secretive. We worked it through contacts. I killed the contacts and worked direct. That's how it was set up.'

'It's true,' said Jim. 'It's how we knew it was tight. Five of us operating, none knowing the other. Jobs just coming, the money coming afterwards as well.'

'The job go out to all of you?' asked Julian.

'No,' said Mike. 'It was handed over one at a time.'

'So, you're the main contact, Mike,' said Julian. 'You're the one everything has to come through. If you're compromised, somebody could step in there. Somebody could get those contact details.'

Mike looked at the floor. 'What are you saying?'

'It's not sitting with me,' said Julian, 'how Alex died. Alex was a hitman, along with the rest of you. Somebody must have discovered who Alex was. Somebody knew who Alex was. Knew how he got his contact. After all, they took him and placed him out in the hermitage in Tollymore. He must have been given a job out there or a contact to meet.'

'Did you know he was a hitman?' asked Siobhan of Susan.

'Didn't know him from Adam. It's only afterwards when they told me the Fox had been hit. When the rumours abounded. I didn't know, did I? If I ever was doing it for the group, I wouldn't have put it out to anyone else. Made me nervous, but then I got the Randolph job. Next, the job for Xavier. Got the feeling I was being rewarded,' said Susan.

'Those jobs came from outside. Contact with possibly the service,' said Mike.

'You really don't know who you're dealing with,' said Julian. 'You've kept yourself so cut off that you're not even sure who you're dealing with.'

'How do you know when you're dealing with the Service?' asked Mike. 'How do you know these people?'

'Because you know them inside out,' said Julian. 'You get hold of somebody who used to be in it. You get hold of several people. You find out these people's faces, names, because we've all done something, and we've all been recognised somewhere.'

'So, someone's playing someone,' said Siobhan.

'I hired the Seafood goons to find him,' said Susan. 'Told me who he was. Told me he was there. Because he wasn't always in that flat. First time I came,' said Susan, 'he wasn't about. I wasn't going to hang about. You want to be coming to a location once, twice at most.'

'So,' said Julian. 'What we know is Kieran's brother died because someone paid Mike to kill him, but Mike doesn't know who.'

'No,' said Mike, 'I told you. It came through the system. I got Xavier, too. Female touch. Then we got you. That went out to everybody. Because I had my reasons for that. Susan should have been there too, but obviously she was with you guys. I didn't realise that. I simply thought she'd failed the first time. I simply thought it hadn't worked out in Belfast. Didn't realise she'd been captured,' said Mike. 'Only when Emma told me. Should have cut and run then. Should have disappeared.'

'Absolutely, you should,' said Julian. 'Prestige, money, something got to your head.'

Kieran looked at them all. 'So you killed my brother.' He shook his head, staring at Susan.

'And then you lot, you were asked to kill these people and you couldn't do that either. I really should never have got involved with such a load of rank amateurs.'

Time almost stood still. Siobhan suddenly clocked what was going on. She saw Kieran reach inside his jacket, pull out a gun and with incredible speed put a bullet in Susan's head. Then Jim, Dave, and then Mike, the weapon was spinning on further, looking to go to Julian.

But as the hand moved round, the room went dark. Lights flashed, and a siren screamed. Siobhan covered her ears and fell to the floor. The disorientation was overwhelming. It was like the room was spinning while a pain was shooting through her head. The sound was incredibly high-pitched, incredibly piercing. It was all she could do to cover her ears and roll into a ball on the floor.

The piercing noise continued, but the lights came on. From the corner of her eye, she saw Kieran, his gun having fallen to the floor. He was rolling up in a ball, covering his ears. Stepping past him, and then on top of him, was Julian.

He rolled the man onto his front, grabbed his arms, cuffed him, and then he jabbed a needle into the back of his neck. Kieran struggled desperately and then went silent.

Julian walked back over and picked up his control unit from the ground. He pressed a button and the screaming sound was switched off. He walked over to Siobhan, helped her sit up, and then made his way to Declan and Kylie.

Kylie's nose was bleeding. Declan looked shocked and completely disorientated. Siobhan pulled herself together and looked over at Julian.

'What the hell?' she said. 'What was—' She turned and looked. The four hitmen were slumped in their chairs, their heads hanging off to one side. In the forehead of each of them, a single bullet hole, blood running out the front.

'It's okay,' said Julian. 'It's okay. We're all okay.'

Chapter 33

Siobhan Duffy ran her hands through her hair, getting out the last of the soap as she stood in the shower. It was good to be back in her house—really good. The safe house was obviously compromised. It had four bodies in it. The three weeks that followed were intense, even if their lives were no longer at stake.

Julian had contacted the Service. With four bodies and a hit man needing to be removed from society, he felt he had little choice; they had operated above the law after all. They had not taken the hit men to the police alive, they instead allowed somebody else to come in and kill them. He was a dangerous person and they couldn't just let him go.

No, the service was the only option; either that or they were going to hand him over to the Fredericks for them to despatch him, or they would have to despatch the man themselves. The Service, however, was very amenable. The Fox had taken out several agents in the past, and they wanted to know something about how it had happened.

They wanted to know about the Fox's connections, so the Service came in. They cleaned up the room, removed the bodies, took away Kieran, and then completely transformed the house, turning it back into a normal dwelling.

A man had arrived one night at the house, and Julian had invited him in, referring to him only as Cecil. There weren't many Cecils around these days, and Siobhan got the idea she wasn't meant to know who he was. Julian knew him though, and the man, with no airs or graces, sat down in the living room to talk to Siobhan. And to Julian. He refused the company of Declan and Kylie.

The conversation had gone as such. The man had interrogated Kieran thoroughly. Julian had suspected that Kieran wasn't Kieran. He, in fact, was Alex. Alex was a true cold-blooded killer. He had set up the hitmen in the Fox group to kill his brother because he wanted them exposed. His elaborate plan had first of all meant offering Kieran, his brother, up.

He'd made contact with him, and got him to stay in the flat. He'd been able to watch all of the goons from the Seafood company come by, identify him, and then pass those details on to a hitman. He didn't know it was going to be Susan for Alex didn't know who the other hitmen were. His plan was to remove them all and take over. He had worked out Mike's new system of passing messages. He'd worked out where they were coming from. They had an IP address and a lot of computer jargon, which Siobhan didn't understand.

The long and the short of it was, he understood how the system worked. So, he could slip in and take over. After Susan had killed his brother, he had posed as Kieran, and come to see Siobhan Duffy.

Her reputation within the community had grown. He knew she could do a job, and he knew she was dogged. So he'd set her up, including the video on Randolph, knowing that she would eventually find Susan. When she did, he then decided she was going to walk away. He'd sent the glitter bomb, making them the target and hiring the Fox to go after them. That was it, his whole plan, to keep Siobhan going so she could expose the other hitmen. And then, after she'd done so, she had presented him with all of them. In fact, it was only Julian's special room that had saved the team, that and his quick reactions. Because in that room, Alex would have killed them all and then walked away with nobody being the wiser.

Siobhan sat feeling rather cold after that conversation. Cecil had asked Julian about Declan's parents and received assurances they would remain quiet. They didn't know who the man was, and they were being told not to tell anyone about the near miss that had happened. Julian believed they would keep quiet for the sake of their son and as they knew nothing, there was nothing more really to say.

Cecil seemed happy with that. When he had left, Siobhan had curled up in Julian's arms. Her body had shaken as he held her. She'd been played. The whole time she'd been played. Her drive, her enthusiasm, her determination to get to the end. Alex had read her, understood her, played her. Julian had said walk away. *He had said walk away.*

The hard bit was the next day, explaining to Declan and Kylie that she was stepping out of the business.

'What do you mean, Mrs D?' Declan had said. 'Sure, that was rough. But we got through it didn't we? We got—'

'I nearly got us all killed, Declan, for God's sake. What are you like? Don't you get that? We were—we were nearly all dead.'

She'd stormed out of the room. It wasn't Declan's fault. He hadn't truly understood. She'd brought Kylie and him into it.

236

She'd heard Kylie berating him but it wasn't Declan's fault. It was hers. She'd brought them in and thank God she'd brought Julian in with them.

When she'd calmed down later in the day, she'd brought both of them in again. She'd asked them if they wanted Gold Coast Investigations to continue. Declan said he enjoyed it. Siobhan said that might have been her problem. She told him she had to step out. Julian brought them together, though.

He suggested that Gold Coast Investigations become a little less dynamic. Take on some cases where husbands were playing around, wives were cheating, domestic issues, things of a lower level. He suggested he would train Declan and Kylie in these things. He would take an executive role in the business while Siobhan took time out. He asked what she was going to do, because she couldn't sit at peace.

'You could get into that garden,' said Declan. Siobhan looked at him.

'Declan, I hired a gardener for that. Do you know why? Because that's not something I'm going to be into. I need something to run. I need something to flourish with.'

'You could, you know, spend your time with Julian,' said Kylie. 'Go out to garden centres. Teas, coffees, lunch.'

Julian looked over at Kylie. 'How well do you know her?' he said. And then he turned to Siobhan. 'Why don't you open up a garden centre?'

'What do you mean?'

'Garden centre, tea, coffee shop. Give you something to do, something to run.'

'I'm not putting tea and coffee in front of people.'

'I didn't mean that. I said run it. Give you something to do during the day. I'll have these two idiots to look after.

237

And, well, we'll have time for ourselves. I think you'll enjoy managing other people. It'll be a challenge, but I don't think you can get anybody killed running a garden centre.'

It wasn't something that appealed to her, but Julian might be right. Maybe she would grow into it. Maybe it was something that would take her fancy. 'And I haven't got the funds,' she said.

'I have,' said Julian. 'Or rather, we have. The Service was pretty delighted at us bringing the Fox in. And they were all so worried about what you've been doing. They said they wanted you to take a back seat somewhere.'

'And you agreed to that?'

'Siobhan, it was the Service. You know what they're like. They had talked about the Bahamas, retiring us out there permanently. I told them you weren't leaving here. This was home. I said I'd be with you.'

'You said you'd look after me? You said you would make sure I wouldn't get back involved?'

Julian laughed. 'Garden centre. They stumped up the money. They were going to pay for it. Well, they were going to pay for whatever I managed to occupy you with.'

'And you didn't think to bring me into the conversation?'

'No,' said Julian, 'because you would have told them to go and stuff it. You would have told them.'

The conversation had been an awkward one in some ways. Declan was happy, and he said he'd advise what plants to get into the centre, what people liked round here. Kylie was just glad everything was winding down. She had enjoyed the investigating, but it had got too crazy. She seemed to have a great trust in Julian and she said she would give it a go along with Declan, now that the Gold Coast investigations were going to be a bit more sedate.

Siobhan let the water cascade over her body. Life was going to start again. She was going to get her life with Julian and she'd have to make it a proper life. She'd be busy. Siobhan also decided she was going to go to a drawing class once a week. She couldn't draw, but she'd have to learn. New challenges. She'd have to keep busy.

She stepped out of the shower, took her towel, and dried herself down in her bedroom. Lying on the bed were her jeans and her favourite jumper. She put on her underwear and dressed in them. If she was going to run a garden centre, she was going to do it on her terms. She'd look as she would look.

The doorbell rang. She smiled. She walked out and opened it to find Julian standing there. 'You are going to move in properly,' she said. 'This is going to be ours. That's my side of the deal. You with me all the time.'

'I have moved in.'

'You said you had, but you hadn't. All your stuff.'

'You don't trust me to be with you.'

'You didn't trust me. That's why all your stuff wasn't in. You gave up everything and you held back on moving everything in because you weren't sure that was going to be enough for me.' She grabbed him by the shirt collar, pulled him towards her. 'You're enough for me. You will be enough for me.'

They kissed until a voice behind them said, 'Get a room.' Kylie barged in.

'Hey, Mrs D, you ready?' Declan was smiling.

'This'll be a lot about the business, Declan. Not just about the flowers.'

'You're dropping us off,' said Kylie. 'We've got to go into the office. Job to do. Julian's going with you.'

'I can come if you need me, though,' said Declan.

'No. It's all right, Declan.'

Siobhan got into the car with Julian. They drove out into the country to a garden centre which hadn't run for two years. She would look around it.

Siobhan stepped out of the car and saw a woman lingering by one of the doors. Siobhan marched over. The woman had a shawl round her head and diamonds on her hands but her back was to Siobhan. But when she turned, Siobhan recognised the face.

'Veronica,' said Siobhan. 'Why are you—'

'Just squaring the circle. Rounding up the loose ends,' said Veronica. 'Been told that you're stepping out.'

'I am.'

'I thought you'd want to know. Emma doesn't work for me anymore.'

'Should that be a concern for us?' asked Julian.

'No,' said Veronica. 'Emma won't be having another job.'

'Thank you for the information,' said Siobhan. 'Just for the record, I don't agree with what your father and his brother did, besides your organisation—'

'I don't think we need to go there. I apologise for the harm we may have put your way, but I think you can keep out of my way, and I will most definitely keep out of yours. Although I may drop by every once in a while to get a minor feature for the garden.'

'I think we know where we stand,' said Julian.

'The woman you want to talk to is inside. I told her I had a bereavement in the family to tell you about. She was very understanding. Like I say, we know where we stand.'

She stepped forward and put her hand out, and Siobhan

shook it. Part of her would love to have brought down Frederick's organisation for all that he did. It was someone else's job. It would have to be. She watched Veronica walk across the car park where a car pulled up. A door was opened for her and she stepped in and drove out of Siobhan's life forever.

'That's that,' said Julian. 'That's really that.'

Siobhan turned, took his hands in hers. 'You know, there's a part of me that wants to take her down. Wants to go through that organisation, rip up all the nonsense.'

'And you don't think there's part of me, too?' said Julian. 'We're fifty. You don't know how long you get. Twenty more years if we're fortunate. Maybe thirty. But the next ten or fifteen is probably when we're going to be the most sprightly we're going to be ever again. There's a ton of wrongs in this world I want to right. But above all that,' said Julian, 'I want to be here with you. I think I've done my time. I think I deserve you.'

'I pledge,' said Siobhan, 'at this garden centre, Gold Coast Investigations will be on the small scale.'

'Deal.'

'You and our life here is all there's going to be unless you want to get back into it.'

'You promise?' asked Julian.

'Yes,' she said. 'You've no idea how hard it is for me to have said that.'

'Oh, I do,' said Julian. 'I know you far too well and you've put it onto me to keep you at this garden centre, to keep you out of the other shenanigans.'

He leaned forward and kissed her on the lips. 'Right then,' he said, 'let's go buy a garden centre.'

241

She took his hand, walked forward and then stopped and turned and looked around her. The rolling hills, the sea in the far-off distance, the greenery. The sky that wasn't completely blue but had rolling clouds that every once in a while dropped some wonderful sunshine. And possibly some rain in the far-off distance. She was home with her man. This is going to be good. It would have to be good enough to quell her restless heart.

Read on to discover the Patrick Smythe series!

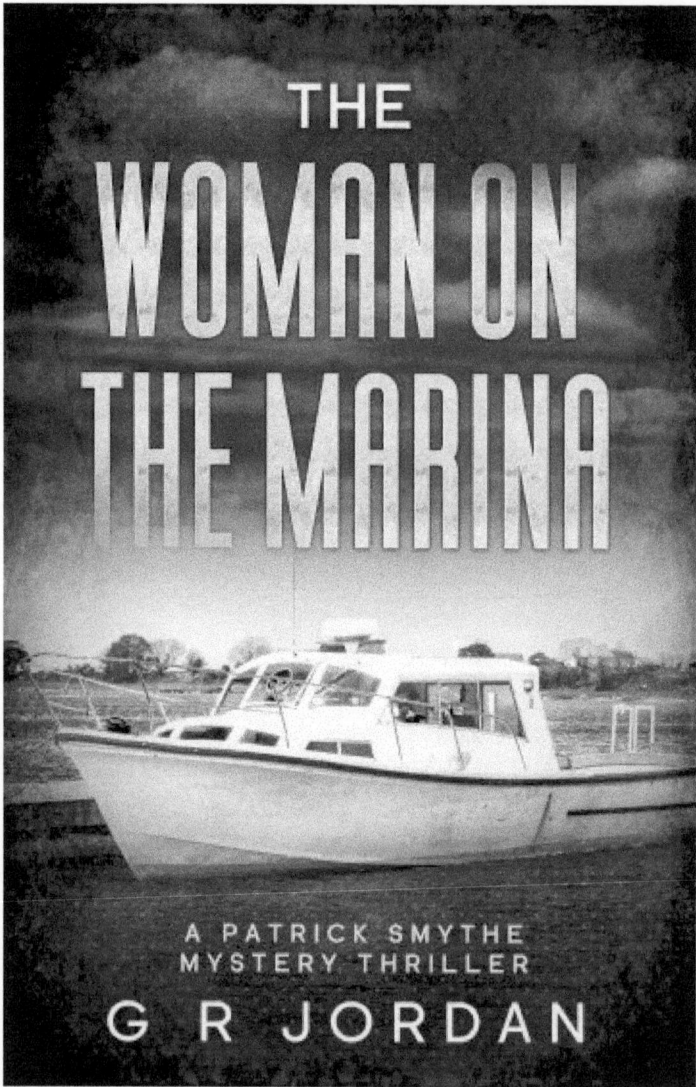

THE
WOMAN ON
THE MARINA

A PATRICK SMYTHE
MYSTERY THRILLER

G R JORDAN

Patrick Smythe is a former Northern Irish policeman who

after suffering an amputation after a bomb blast, takes to the sea between the west coast of Scotland and his homeland to ply his trade as a private investigator. Join Paddy as he tries to work to his own ethics while knowing how to bend the rules he once enforced. Working from his beloved motorboat 'Craigantlet', Paddy decides to rescue a drug mule in this short story from the pen of G R Jordan.

Join G R Jordan's monthly newsletter about forthcoming releases and special writings for his tribe of avid readers and then receive your free Patrick Smythe short story.

Go to https://bit.ly/PatrickSmythe for your Patrick Smythe journey to start!

About the Author

G R Jordan is a self-published author who finally decided at forty that in order to have an enjoyable lifestyle, his creative beast within would have to be unleashed. His books mirror that conflict in life where acts of decency contend with self-promotion, goodness stares in horror at evil, and kindness blindsides us when we at our worst. Corrupting our world with his parade of wondrous and horrific characters, he highlights everyday tensions with fresh eyes whilst taking his methodical, intelligent mainstays on a roller-coaster ride of dilemmas, all the while suffering the banter of their provocative sidekicks.

A graduate of Loughborough University where he masqueraded as a chemical engineer but ultimately played American football, Gary had worked at changing the shape of cereal flakes and pulled a pallet truck for a living. Watching vegetables freeze at -40'C was another career highlight and he was also one of the Scottish Highlands "blind" air traffic controllers.

These days he has graduated to answering a telephone to people in trouble before telephoning other people to sort it out.

Having flirted with most places in the UK, he is now based in the Isle of Lewis in Scotland where his free time is spent between raising a young family with his wife, writing, figuring out how to work a loom and caring for a small flock of chickens. Luckily, his writing is influenced by his varied work and life experience as the chickens have not been the poetical inspiration he had hoped for!

You can connect with me on:

- https://grjordan.com
- https://facebook.com/carpetlessleprechaun

Subscribe to my newsletter:

- https://bit.ly/PatrickSmythe

Also by G R Jordan

G R Jordan writes across multiple genres including crime, dark and action adventure fantasy, feel good fantasy, mystery thriller and horror fantasy. Below is a selection of his work. Whilst all books are available across online stores, signed copies are available at his personal shop.

Highlands and Islands Detective Thriller Series
https://grjordan.com/product/waters-edge
Join stalwart DI Macleod and his burgeoning new DC McGrath as they look into the darker side of the stunningly scenic and wilder parts of the north of Scotland. From the Black Isle to Lewis, from Mull to Harris and across to the small Isles, the Uists and Barra, this mismatched pairing follow murders, thieves and vengeful victims in an effort to restore tranquillity to the remoter parts of the land.

Be part of this tale of a surprise partnership amidst the foulest deeds and darkest souls who stalk this peaceful and most beautiful of lands, and you'll never see the Highlands the same way again.

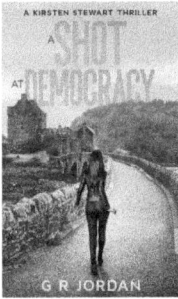

Kirsten Stewart Thrillers

https://grjordan.com/product/a-shot-at-democracy

Join Kirsten Stewart on a shadowy ride through the underbelly of the Highlands of Scotland where among the beauty and splendour of the majestic landscape lies corruption and intrigue to match any city. From murders to extortion, missing children to criminals operating above the law, the Highland former detective must learn a tougher edge to her work as she puts her own life on the line to protect those who cannot defend themselves.

Having left her beloved murder investigation team far behind, Kirsten has to battle personal tragedy and loss while adapting to a whole new way of executing her duties where your mistakes are your own. As Kirsten comes to terms with working with the new team, she often operates as the groups solo field agent, placing herself in danger and trouble to rescue those caught on the dark side of life. With action packed scenes and tense scenarios of murder and greed, the Kirsten Stewart thrillers will have you turning page after page to see your favourite Scottish lass home!

There's life after Macleod, but a whole new world of death!

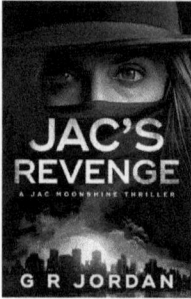

Jac's Revenge (A Jack Moonshine Thriller #1)
https://grjordan.com/product/jacs-revenge
An unexpected hit makes Debbie a widow. The attention of her man's killer spawns a brutal yet classy alter ego. But how far can you play the game before it takes over your life?

All her life, Debbie Parlor lived in her man's shadow, knowing his work was never truly honest. She turned her head from news stories and rumours. But when he was disposed of for his smile to placate a rival crime lord, Jac Moonshine was born. And when Debbie is paid compensation for her loss like her car was written off, Jac decides that enough is enough.

Get on board with this tongue-in-cheek revenge thriller that will make you question how far you would go to avenge a loved one, and how much you would enjoy it!

Milton Keynes UK
Ingram Content Group UK Ltd.
UKHW041048150824
446997UK00001B/13

9 781915 562845